THE VERMEER CONSPIRACY

THE
Vermeer
Conspiracy

EYTAN HALABAN

PORTLAND • OREGON
INKWATERPRESS.COM

*Scan this QR Code
to learn more about
this title*

Halaban, Eytan, 1936-
    The Vermeer conspiracy / by Eytan Halaban.
    pages cm
    LCCN 2015904647
    ISBN 978-1-62901-239-1 (pbk.)
    ISBN 978-1-62901-240-7 (Kindle ebk.)
    ISBN 978-1-62901-241-4 (epub ebk.)

    1. Women art historians--Fiction. 2. Vermeer, Johannes, 1632-1675--Fiction. 3. Conspiracy theories--Fiction. I. Title.

    PR9510.9.H27V47 2015   823'.914
                        QBI15-600084

Publisher: Inkwater Press | www.inkwaterpress.com

Paperback ISBN-13 978-1-62901-239-1 | ISBN-10 1-62901-239-4
Kindle ISBN-13 978-1-62901-240-7 | ISBN-10 1-62901-240-8
ePub ISBN-13 978-1-62901-241-4 | ISBN-10 1-62901-241-6

Printed in the U.S.A.

3 5 7 9 10 8 6 4 2

To Ruth. Always.

And to the Amazing Four Halabans,
Zoe, Tobias, Jonah and Penelope.

To my Editor:

The title "My Editor" is too narrow to describe the help and the contribution of my editor, Lauren Simpson. Lauren edited, cut, added and corrected the manuscript in its many incarnations, and she did it with wit and humor and enormous patience. My deepest thanks.

THE VERMEER CONSPIRACY

I TOLD THE POLICE EVERYTHING I KNEW ABOUT DANIELLE.

During the first session, the two detectives were polite, especially the older one, who took on the sympathetic uncle role. Once they held the door open for me and escorted me back to the elevator, I'd assumed my part was finished and I could go on speculating about what had happened to my roommate.

But then the dean informed me that the detectives wanted to speak with me again.

I explained, once again, careful not to repeat the same phrases. Danielle and I were close friends, though I had barely known her name when we agreed to live together sophomore year, both of us stranded without roommates and at the wrong end of the room draw lottery. We'd paired up with two other girls who kept their extra sheets at our place and their clothes at their boyfriends', and that had been that. Our arrangement of convenience worked, and Danielle and I had been roommates ever since—at least, until September of our senior year, when she vanished.

Danielle and I had little in common, not even academic interests. She declared art history as her major from the get-go, and as I quickly found out, if given the chance, Danielle would go on for hours about the subject of her passion, the seventeenth-century Dutch painter Carel Fabritius. One night early in our acquaintance, she'd let slip over a box of Franzia that her parents owned a Fabritius—not a high-quality reproduction, but an actual Fabritius canvas, a little-known depiction of a cluttered painter's studio. Danielle loved the painting so much that she'd hired a photographer to make a poster reproduction, which now hung over her side of our bedroom. As my childhood home was adorned with a selection of inoffensive paintings picked up at T.J. Maxx, I'd kept my mouth shut and my wine glass full.

Unlike Danielle, I oscillated among majors—premed, econ, math, socio-economics, psychology—and amassed the required classes for each. Finally, on the last possible date sophomore year, I decided on astronomy, but only because I loved the math. Danielle couldn't see the beauty in the numbers, but then, to be fair, I couldn't see what the fuss over Fabritius was all about.

For a second time, the detectives listened to me talk, prodding when my words petered out, then shook my hand and let me leave their broom closet of an interview room. I didn't realize I'd taken my cold coffee with me until I was three blocks away.

MY DEAN COACHED ME TO simply tell the truth when he informed me that the police wanted to interview me for a third time. "I'm sure this is just routine," he told me as I stood in the corner of his office, feeling sick to my stomach. His eyes suggested otherwise.

"Should I get a lawyer?" I mumbled.

"Do you think you need one?" he asked in reply, clasping his hands over a stack of papers and staring too intently at my face.

I was scared, yes, but I was still angry—angry with the police for treating me like a suspect, angry with my dean for taking their side, angry with Danielle forever going to New York in the first place—and so, once again, I went to the police department alone.

The coffee was the same, lukewarm and vile, but the conversation had shifted closer to interrogation than simple questioning. Still, I held my composure and matched the detectives' hard stares. At one point, the "good cop," now showing the edge beneath his avuncular façade, asked if I were envious of Danielle.

I studied his eager eyes for a moment, then shrugged. "Of course."

He tensed, perhaps imagining that he was having his own Perry Mason moment. "Oh? Why's that?"

"Who *wouldn't* be?" I replied, hoping a touch of scorn would make his excitement deflate. The question had been stupid, the answer obvious.

Danielle was a natural beauty with an easy grace. She played the piano like she was born at the keys and passed her classes with only occasional glances at her stack of expensive textbooks. The rich scion of a long line of Yale graduates, Danielle was a legacy multiple times over, and she fit the stereotype of the country club set.

I was a full four inches shorter than Danielle, dark-haired, and muscular from years of soccer practice. There had been no country club in my past. I was on full scholarship, the only child of a Colombian mother who worked two jobs and a Caucasian father who'd never laid eyes on me. Quiet and stocky, easy to dismiss and, most humiliating, easy to underestimate. Not being taken seriously had always been part of my existence.

Danielle was certain of everything. I was sure of nothing.

I could go on and on listing the differences between us. Shopping trips to the City, invitations to dances and dinners, professors' attention—she had plenty, and I had almost none. All I could boast of was my superior ability to recall details; I have an almost photographic memory that at times made Danielle envious of me. But in those years of our acquaintance, I would have traded all the recall in the world for a chance to live Danielle's charmed life.

The detective wavered, but only briefly. "Do you like her?"

"Sure." They maintained their tactical pause, waiting for me to expand on my answer, and I fought back frustrated tears. "She's always been kind to me."

I had nothing to do with her disappearance, I wanted to scream, but I knew futility when I saw it.

The younger detective rubbed his shoulder against the air-conditioned chill of the interview room. "In what way was she kind to you?"

"She was just a kind person," I said, avoiding his stare so as not to show him tears, then realized I'd slipped into the past tense. "She *is* a kind person."

He hadn't reacted to my slip, but I still didn't trust his eyes. "Go on."

I sighed and glanced into my coffee cup. "You want an

example? Okay. She took me home with her for Thanks-giving sophomore year."

The detectives cut their eyes to each other. "That sounds nice," the younger replied. "But you didn't want to go home for the holiday? See your folks?"

I stared at him until he looked down at his notepad.

THERE'S A SCENE IN *A Christmas Carol* that inevitably takes me back to freshman year. Ebenezer Scrooge, cantankerous as always, has been brought through time to his boyhood school. There, he watches in joy as his former classmates ride off for home and the holiday—and then he finds his younger self alone, reading by the fire, and sobs.

I was the only person in my four-story entryway with nowhere to go for Thanksgiving that year. Even the foreign students had planned out-of-town trips and mass dinners at apartments off campus. Of my sextet, I alone remained in the dorm, missing home terribly but playing it off as no big deal. Mom was working on Thanksgiving, anyway, I told my suitemates, and besides, an Amtrak ride back to Chicago would be an expensive, protracted pain. I insisted I would be fine as they made their separate departures, and then, when all I could hear was the building settling around me, I had a good cry. I'd spent Thanksgiving afternoon curled up on our sagging communal futon with a bucket of Popeye's and the National Dog Show, promising myself I'd save enough for a ticket next year.

And then next year was upon me, and once more, I was strapped for cash. I kept the matter to myself, and of course, I said nothing to Danielle. We both had projects to finish, and any conversation turned to The Game on Saturday in

Cambridge, our projected trouncing, and rumors of viewing parties for those unwilling to make the trek north. Not until the Friday before, when Danielle realized she was the only one of us with a suitcase out of the closet, did she learn that my holiday plans didn't involve home.

"What do you mean, you're staying here?" she asked, pausing in her struggle with her overstuffed bag's zipper. "It's Thanksgiving!"

"And it's a week of peace and quiet," I replied, not looking up from my computer, a clunky desktop model that took up most of my workspace. "I've got a paper due first of December in my history of science seminar, and"—I scrolled to the end of the document—"I'm still a good twenty pages shy, even if I get creative with the margins. I'll be fine," I added, looking up in time to catch her look of incredulity. "Really. It's okay."

"Forget it. You're coming home with me," she insisted. "I'll be in Boston this weekend, but I'll return Monday, and we'll go over to my parents' place Thursday morning. Stay the night and be back on campus Friday—you'll have plenty of time to write!"

Danielle, in her way, made it seem as if I were the one doing her the favor by gracing the table with my presence. When my half-hearted protests failed to change her mind, I threw a nice dress into a bag, dug out a decent pair of pajamas, and tried to find something new to say about Einstein that weekend while the campus settled down into its post-defeat, pre-holiday lull.

DANIELLE LIVED IN WESTPORT, A forty-minute drive from New Haven, and her home was the largest I had ever entered.

I tried not to gawk, but I couldn't help it. The indoor pool, the marble floors, the wide, semicircular staircase with Venetian cast-iron banisters, the Dutch masterpieces on the walls, and the crystal chandeliers—its elegance, like Danielle's, was effortless. Twenty-eight people, family and their guests, filled the house with happy conversation and the clatter of cutlery, while two cooks and three servers kept the dishes coming. Even with the crowd, I had a guestroom to myself, giving me an escape from the well-meaning crowd of strangers.

Early in the afternoon, while the punchbowl was being refreshed and the tray of chilled shrimp picked apart, I was exploring the house to keep from underfoot when I wandered into the library. My eye initially went to the black baby grand and the wall of leather-bound books—there were no paperbacks on the Carruthers' shelves, nothing so pedestrian—but when I turned away to press on with my self-guided tour, I spotted a familiar painting hanging above an antique yew side table: the beloved Fabritius, hanging in the open, illuminated by the soft glow of a museum-style brass lamp. On instinct, I reached out to feel the canvas, but I restrained myself and peered closer at the painted chaos, the covered canvas on the easel in the left corner, the green tree spilling through the window on the left side, the model, young and somberly dressed, staring out at the viewer. There was something pleasing in the painting's architecture, something almost harmonious in the mess of what I could only assume was good old Carel Fabritius's studio. True, the man needed a maid, but he'd managed to capture something exquisite in his model's face, a demure smile with a hint of shyness beneath. Was this her first sitting, I wondered, and if so, how did she feel being plopped into the middle of a strange man's workshop and instructed not to move?

I had studied the painting for a few minutes, trying to imagine it hanging on a wall of my mother's two-bedroom apartment, when Danielle walked by and caught me. "It's better up close, isn't it?" she said, joining me. "My grandfather bought it in Delft."

"It's really an original?" I asked, and immediately felt foolish.

"It better be," she said, almost laughing. "He never allowed reproductions in his house." She reached up where I hadn't dared and brushed her pale fingertips against the heavy frame. Her touch was sensuous, the moment reverent, and for a fleeting instant, I thought she might kiss her fingertips when she slowly pulled her hand away. "Vermeer touched that frame, you know," she whispered. "Maybe even Rembrandt. Can you imagine what that painting has seen?"

THE NEXT MORNING, I WOKE to a silent house and, for lack of a better idea, continued my tour. I roamed the halls, listening to my footsteps echo in the stillness. Rooming with Danielle, I'd had no idea of just how wealthy she was—she never spoke about it, and I'd only gotten hints from the labels in her closet. As I crept down the main staircase, I half expected to be passed by a young woman in a dark dress and white apron, the sort of creature who'd press herself to the wall, bob a curtsey, and wish me good morning in a cockney accent.

Roaming in awe, I turned my steps toward the back of the house and emerged through French doors onto a wide veranda overlooking a rolling meadow. Not one blade of grass was out of place, and the oaks by the distant brook stood thick and proud, ancient beside the saplings that struggled to survive on the street outside my mother's tenement building. As I took in the cool morning, I spotted Danielle's mother sitting in a wicker chair on the other side of the veranda, surrounded by *The New York Times*, a stack of magazines, and a cup of coffee.

"Over here, Sabrina," she called with a smile, and invited me to join her with an elegant wave of her hand—Danielle's hand, twenty years removed. When I approached, I saw a yellow legal pad on her lap. Her face was flawless, her clothing immaculate even at that hour, and I thought of my exhausted mother, who was almost certainly already at work, trying to manage the madness of Black Friday.

"I always start my Christmas list the day after Thanksgiving," Mrs. Carruthers said, and patted the empty seat beside her. "Now, what would you like for Christmas, dear?"

I burst into tears.

Of course, I didn't tell the detectives all of that. I just summed up the visit, recounting how kind and warm it had been. They wanted to see the leather knapsack Danielle's mother had bought me for Christmas not so much out of curiosity, I assumed, but as a detective's reflex, corroborating a detail of my story. I didn't tell them that it was the most expensive thing I owned, just as I didn't mention Danielle and Fabritius.

"Did you know anybody else, another guest or guests?" asked the sympathetic uncle, whose sympathy was wearing quite thin.

I knew to whom he referred, and I answered without hesitation. "Yes. Whitmore Verhaast."

His eyebrow quirked upward. "Friend of yours?"

"No, he's Danielle's senior essay adviser. I think he was Mr. Carruthers's classmate at Yale."

"Ah. A family friend, then? Is that why Danielle was working with him?"

I didn't fall into the trap. I knew that Professor Verhaast had been on their list, and most likely had been already interviewed. "She's his student," I said, shrugging—what else was there to say to a detective? "Danielle loves the Dutch Masters. Verhaast's an expert on the subject. I'm pretty sure she would have gone to him, family friend or not." They employed their tactical silence once more, and I filled the gap with the same nonchalant shrug. "He's been her mentor for a few years, and he's her adviser now. That's all."

That was a lie, of course. I didn't tell them about the rumor that Danielle had an affair with Verhaast; the detectives had probably heard it already, precipitating their question. Such rumors were a constant tail to Verhaast and to any female student—or junior female professor, for that matter—who came into his orbit. Verhaast was one of those luminaries who made Yale Yale, a bright comet towing lesser luminaries in his glowing wake, but his personal reputation was less than stellar. Then again, Verhaast was tall and athletic, with a hint of silver in his thick black hair, a turtleneck and impeccable blazer, eyes that kissed you, and a deep voice that embraced you—small wonder that such rumors endured.

I could tell the two detectives wanted to hear me expand on the subject, but I just shrugged again.

I didn't tell them that Verhaast's notoriety wasn't just a

rumor. I didn't tell them about my freshman year, my private and constant pain. I didn't tell them about the abortion he paid for, or the way he had done his best to ignore me at Danielle's house.

And I also didn't tell them about the sweeping performance Verhaast had put on about the Fabritius in the library during cocktails before Thanksgiving dinner. As always, he had mesmerized his audience—there was no denying that the man had a gift for public speaking, even if he was a sleazy bastard. If the detectives had seen the way Danielle looked at that painting while Verhaast was lecturing, and saw the way Verhaast looked at Danielle in turn, they wouldn't have doubted that the two were more than just teacher and student.

I wanted to believe that their affair wasn't physical. Danielle was stronger than that. Theirs was a sensual sort of platonic affair, fired by their mutual passion for seventeenth-century Dutch paintings, which, at least that evening, boiled in the presence of the Fabritius.

I happened to catch Danielle's eyes in the gilded mirror hanging beside the painting when Verhaast mentioned in deliberate passing the name of Fabritius's protégé and mistress, Hanna Deursen. An unmistakable explosion ignited in her eyes, a flicker of lightning that leapt between master and student, and it had caught me by surprise that the mysterious woman in Fabritius's life could stir such emotion in Danielle. When Verhaast mentioned Deursen again—"I'd give half my kingdom for five minutes with her," he said with a little laugh—Danielle's eyes reflected a nearly maddening rage. But the moment passed, and Verhaast quickly switched to Vermeer and Dutch paintings in general. Danielle's eyes returned to their usual warm hazel light, and

Verhaast didn't mention Deursen again. But I saw that madness, and I moved closer to my roommate, silently taking her hand as Verhaast continued his gin-fueled monologue.

THE POLICE QUESTIONED VERHAAST, AS they did all of Danielle's professors and friends. Many of the questions the detectives threw at me were traps to ensnare discrepancies in my testimony or to corroborate details in others. Apparently, Verhaast didn't mention Fabritius or Deursen; he wasn't asked, and neither was I.

I told the detectives everything I knew about Danielle—her habits, her friends, her love for strawberry-topped Belgian waffles on Saturday mornings in the dining hall—but on the most important topic, I kept my silence. By then, I knew too much, and I had begun to fear the worst.

T HE WEEK THAT DANIELLE FAILED TO RETURN FROM HER TRIP to New York, Verhaast was on a lecture tour in Europe. When he returned, the police were already swarming the campus, but he had a perfect alibi. I, on the other hand, had been the last to see her, and I was the one who reported her missing.

At the end of our third session together, the two detectives asked me whether any of Danielle's belongings had been left in our room. I reminded them that the state's forensic unit had combed the place twice and confiscated her things, and that the police had taken her iPad; her laptop, I told them, had been with her when she took the train to New York.

"Are you sure about that?" they'd asked.

I'd nodded. "That laptop goes everywhere with her."

"Not the tablet?" the younger asked with a hint of disbelief.

"The tablet is her glorified Game Boy," I snapped. "She was going to New York to get some work done—she wanted a keyboard."

Seemingly satisfied for the moment, the detectives instructed me not to leave town, explaining that they might call me back for further questioning.

"Am I a suspect?" I asked.

They kept their tactical silence.

THAT NIGHT, I STUDIED THE file folder Danielle had labeled "Senior Essay" for the third time since the police had officially declared her missing.

The folder was thick, the pages within neatly labeled, numbered, and dated in Danielle's round and precise handwriting, the envy of any archivist or curator. Small Post-It notes marked important points on each document, each numbered and cross-referenced to a corresponding file in a folder on her laptop called "Hanna Deursen." That folder was the only one on the computer that required a password to open. I hadn't found the password yet, but I was patient. I knew that in the mass of files and folders I had moved from Danielle's desk to mine before the police arrived, I would find a sticker or a note in her perfect handwriting bearing the information I sought.

As was her habit, Danielle had lent me her laptop before she headed to New York. My old desktop model, salvaged from my mother's coworker's basement, was slow and kept me confined to the room while I studied, and Danielle thought I needed to see daylight more often. When the police came to paw through her belongings, I simply neglected to inform them of the laptop's true owner. Of course Danielle had taken her laptop to New York, I told them—this one was mine. The desktop was just there to process telescope data, nothing of importance to them.

The "Hanna Deursen" folder wasn't large, but not knowing its contents kept me awake at night. I had no idea how to get around the password protection, and asking my computer science friends for help wouldn't have been the wisest course of action, considering the circumstances. Instead, I combed the paper file Danielle had left behind, hoping for the needle in that haystack to prick my finger.

LET ME DIGRESS FOR A moment. I was less than fully candid with the investigators not because I was trying to cover my tracks—I had none to cover—but because I knew in my gut that Verhaast was involved in Danielle's disappearance, and I could imagine no sweeter moment in my life than the moment that I exposed him.

Verhaast had hurt me badly. I was eighteen then, poor and insecure, a confused Latina freshman in search of guidance. He had answered my questions, awed me with his brilliance, made me feel special and gifted, like I *belonged*.

And then, one evening, he took me on his office couch.

Welcome to the Ivy League.

THE *YALE DAILY NEWS*, THE undergraduate paper, made me a sort of celebrity on campus. They interviewed me twice, once when Danielle's disappearance baffled but failed to alarm us, and the second time three weeks later when the police showed up. I agreed to be interviewed because failing to do so would only have made me seem shifty in the public eye, and my classmates were already giving me a wider than usual berth—all but Josh, sweet Josh, who continued to bring me cookies and beg for my help on problem sets.

At least the *YDN* sent a friend to do the honors. Brian

Johnston knew Danielle and me well—he was our upstairs neighbor in Entryway L, and we had joined him and his friends on occasion for Friday night pre-gaming prior to going out. We met in my room for privacy, and as I settled onto the couch—not my freshman futon, but a proper sofa donated by the Carruthers—I could tell that Brian was scanning the common room, cataloguing the things the police had taken with them.

"Sit down," I offered, patting the cushion beside me. "Want a Coke or something? I've got beer."

"Beer wouldn't be the most professional tactic, I'm afraid," he said, smiling wistfully as he accepted the red can I handed him. "But thanks anyway, Sabrina." He popped the top, sipped, and absently set the can on our white IKEA coffee table, my meager contribution to the décor. "Let's get this started," he said, and tapped his phone's screen until I saw a red "record" button appear. "This is Monday, September twenty-second, 2014. The time is three-thirty-seven, and I'm here with Sabrina Gutierrez. Sabrina, okay if I record this?"

"Uh, sure," I mumbled, unsure if I really had an option.

Brian led me through the basics, asking some of the same questions the detectives had posed, albeit without their thinly-veiled suspicion. I answered honestly, though I kept the conversation well away from Verhaast and Danielle's involvement with him.

Eventually, Brian picked up his Coke again and gave me a knowing grin. "So, this trip to New York—was she seeing someone new?"

"Would you take a laptop on a date?" I retorted, and he returned to the script.

Our second meeting was at the *YDN* office. Brian sat at

the other end of a long table and kept the recording phone between us. Gone were the flippant questions about my roommate's relationship status, replaced with a new intensity I'd rarely seen in my neighbor. Again, we went over the last few hours of Danielle's time in New Haven, culminating in her Metro-North ticket.

He drummed his fingers on the wooden tabletop and blinked slowly. "So when she goes on these research trips, where does she go?" he asked.

I thought back over our last conversation. "Well, she usually goes to one of the museums. Danielle mentioned that she had an appointment with someone at the Met, but I don't know if she kept it. I mean, that's all I know—I didn't exactly get an itinerary."

"So you're not worried, then?"

He caught me by surprise, and I stared at him over my coffee, shocked and hurt. "Of course I'm worried!" I yelled down the table. "Why wouldn't I be worried? She hasn't picked up the fucking phone in weeks, and I'm *scared*, Brian. Okay? Is that clear enough for you?"

When he printed the story, he was smart enough not to mention my tears.

I TOLD NEITHER BRIAN NOR the police that at the end of our junior year, Danielle returned from a meeting with Verhaast, shouted, "Bastard!" as she slammed the door, then threw herself facedown on her bed and sobbed soundlessly. Only her shoulders trembled. When she finally rolled over and turned to me, her red eyes were ablaze, not with anguish, but with anger—the same angry blaze I had registered when Verhaast mentioned Hanna Deursen at Thanksgiving the year before.

"That prick wants me to drop my research," she spat. "He warned me..."

She stopped abruptly and changed the subject, but she'd confirmed what I feared. I knew then that Danielle and I had a common ravager, but I wasn't yet sure whether her case constituted rape.

The answer was somewhere in that password-protected folder, and the key was surely buried in Danielle's papers. For her sake and mine, I kept them hidden away.

WEEKS AFTER VERHAAST RAPED ME, months before I met Danielle, I started to collect bits of information about him— newspaper clippings, scholarly papers, articles in Yale bulletins, anything bearing his name. At moments of deep pain and anger and helplessness, I would delve six or seven pages into Google, then cut and print and store what I uncovered with only a vague idea of my purpose in doing so. That collection had swollen over the years and now required a small filing cabinet of its own. As I had neither the money nor the space in my dorm room for a proper cabinet, a plastic milk crate from the kitchen served my purposes. I kept it under my bed, and thus, it also escaped the police's notice when they carted away Danielle's stuff.

In my obsessive search to get even with Verhaast, I came upon a ten-year-old story in an Irish newspaper. An art critic and researcher from a small town in Ireland, Didrika Margrit Aken, had travelled to Amsterdam to interview the luminary Professor Verhaast. A week later, on her way back home via Paris, she disappeared without a trace. Her papers, notes, files, all vanished. The French police never suspected a connection between the interview with Verhaast and her disappearance, and neither did I, when I first read the piece. But now, after Danielle's disappearance, one sentence in the last paragraph of the story loomed ominously large and dark:

> *According to family members, Ms Aken was returning from a trip to Amsterdam where she interviewed Whitmore Verhaast, an expert in seventeenth-century Dutch paintings, for an upcoming book on the lives of Delft painters Fabritius and Vermeer.*

Aken's disappearance generated a few references on Google, all were from her hometown newspaper, rehashing the same information.

Verhaast, on the other hand, was all over the news at the time of Aken's disappearance. He was chairing a panel of experts that the Dutch government had convened to verify and authenticate three canvases, two attributed to Rembrandt and the third to Vermeer. In the balance was more than two hundred million dollars. The three canvases were part of the loot the Nazis had stolen, and now, years later, the pieces were returning to their rightful owners. The two Rembrandts were taken from an art collector in Amsterdam whose descendants were scattered all over the world, mostly in the U.S., while the Vermeer was taken from a vacation home by the sea. Neither the house nor any living person connected with it could be located. Verhaast published a monograph on the panel's work, which I had in my collection; he wrote at length about the panel's deliberation and methods and, in less detail but in unambiguous terms, its conclusion. The two Rembrandts were authenticated as the master's work and returned to the family, while the Vermeer was deemed an imitation by an inferior painter, a dilettante of the same period.

Not a word was written thereafter about the fate of the defunct Vermeer, not even a footnote. The canvas, like Danielle and Ms. Aken, had vanished.

TWO WEEKS BEFORE THE END OF THE SEMESTER AND ALMOST eight after the police had declared Danielle missing, just as most of the campus was returning from Thanksgiving break and diving into finals, Verhaast was scheduled to give a lecture for the alumni association's public education program. He kept the appointment, and so did I. My studying was complete, after all—I'd spent another Thanksgiving on campus, finding all kind of excuses to deflect Josh's invitations—Danielle was gone, and my heart was far away from celebration. The pain in Mrs. Carruthers's voice was heart wrenching every time she called, and I felt horribly guilty to have had Danielle's papers for so long and still be no closer to finding her.

3

Verhaast was the scab I loved to pick. I had dropped his class first semester freshman year, shortly after he raped me, but I accompanied Danielle to his public lectures. She'd always sit in the first or second row, and I sat beside her, taking pleasure in staring at

Verhaast the entire time and hoping to make him uncomfortable. For this December lecture, however, I arrived at the Art Gallery's auditorium early to secure a seat in the rear, where I was sure he wouldn't spot me.

The room was, as usual, packed. The title, "Vermeer's Women and the Use of Light in Dutch Paintings," was enticing enough to draw a crowd of students, faculty, and alumni, and even a few retirees from the community. Verhaast was well known, after all, and his lecture had been advertised in *The New York Times*, thanks to his PR agency. Of course, I'd never seen him give a lecture without substantial publicity beforehand—a Yale professor's salary, especially in the humanities, couldn't support his lavish standard of living, and rumor had it that he commanded ten thousand dollars per speaking engagement.

I didn't doubt it, but thanks to my research, I knew another source of his income. Each time that Verhaast was hired to verify and authenticate a canvas, he received a hefty fee as well as a percentage of the subsequent sale. In a few cases, he'd received six-figure payment for his work. Following the trails led me to the realization that Verhaast must keep large sums of money in Europe. For a time, I thought that would be my leverage in getting even with him, but I had no way of knowing whether he had declared this income and reported his foreign bank accounts—and then Danielle disappeared.

I WAS FAMILIAR WITH VERHAAST'S typical public lectures, a variation on the theme: Fabritius's departure from his master, Rembrandt, in technique and use of light, and his influence on Vermeer. Rembrandt, Fabritius, Vermeer—almost a formula to pack auditoriums among the art history set. It was also a central theme in the numerous articles and books he had published. But now, I went to the Art Gallery to listen to his well-oiled lecture through the prism of Danielle's disappearance, to catch a nuance, to detect a deflection in the voice, a gesture in the body, anything that might give me a clue.

Verhaast made his usual bombastic entry like a whirling dervish, pulling behind him his retinue of assistants, postdoctoral fellows, and other admirers. Tall, handsome, and commanding as ever, he nodded approval to the packed hall, then signaled to the projection booth in the back of the auditorium. The light dimmed, he paused, and my heart sank.

He saw me.

Our eyes locked.

I mentally kicked myself. In his classes, Verhaast used PowerPoint presentations from his laptop and changed slides with a remote. In his public lectures, however, he used an assistant to handle the slides. I had foolishly picked a seat in the last row below the tinted glass window of the projection booth, and I had no doubt that Verhaast was staring at me and not at the booth above my head. A second later, he called to the booth, "Veronica, I revised the lecture this morning. I'll use my laptop."

The lights slowly brightened.

"That's okay, keep the lights down," he called while connecting his computer.

The light dimmed, and Verhaast began his revised lecture—addressing, I had no doubt, only me.

THIS TIME, HE DWELT LONGER than usual on the social connection between Fabritius and Vermeer. Usually, he treated the subject with light strokes—just one sentence about how they both lived and worked in Delft—but now he applied detailed touches as he discussed their friendship. Fabritius

View of Delft by Johannes Vermeer

and Vermeer were neighbors in Delft, practically living on the same street. Although there was a ten-year gap in their ages, it was logical to assume that they had friends in common among the artistic community. Beyond their shared interest in painting, Vermeer sold canvasses through the family business—and as he also ran a popular inn near Fabritius's studio, it was almost certain that the two men were more than mere acquaintances. They surely knew the same women, Verhaast told the audience with a wink. "Maybe they shared the same procuress," he added, and winked again. The audience ate it up. Fabritius and Vermeer had joined the Guild of St. Luke, the Delft painters' guild, a year apart—first Fabritius, and then Vermeer, paying half the dues. Both had borrowed the money to do so. "Perhaps from the same benefactress," Verhaast said, and this time, the wink was in his voice.

"But their friendship was short-lived," he continued. "On the morning of October twelfth, 1654"—Verhaast was practically speaking in Italics now and staring at me—"Fabritius died in the famous Delft Explosion, 'the Thunderclap.' A massive gunpowder store ignited and exploded, leveling half the town and killing and maiming hundreds." He employed one of his tactical pauses, letting that fact sink in.

He blinked slowly, then clicked on the first slide.

A picture of Egbert van der Poel's *A View of Delft After the Explosion of 1654* appeared on the screen.

A View of Delft after the Explosion of 1654 by Egbert van der Poel

Verhaast didn't use the slide to show van der Poel's masterful use of shadows to express the devastation, but rather to emphasize the utter destruction. "From our point of view, it was as bad as the Allied bombing of Munich and Danzig after World War II"—he pronounced the name of the cities in German and with a perfect, albeit affected, German accent—"and it destroyed much of the beauty and the art treasures of these cities. The Delft Thunderclap killed Fabritius and undoubtedly incinerated many of his canvases. We don't know where Vermeer was at the time of the explosion, but thank God he wasn't in Delft," Verhaast concluded.

Then his rich baritone changed colors, indicating an anecdote or a secret he was about to share with the audience. "Vermeer was twenty-two at the time. Who'd venture to guess where a vibrant lad of twenty-two spends his time?" The audience tittered. "But this isn't the subject of my talk this morning," Verhaast continued, then stared at me again and clicked the remote.

A portrait of a mangled woman replaced the van der Poel. Her face was deformed: one eye was a black socket, her neck was covered with raised red blotches, her nose was missing, and her mouth was torn into a half-smile. I had never seen that painting, and the auditorium fell into a deep silence.

A beat.

Girl with Pearl Earring by
Johannes Vermeer

"Oops, wrong slide, excuse me, ladies and gentlemen," said Verhaast.

I was familiar with the "wrong slide" trick, which he employed to keep the desired image in the collective mind of his audience. He stared at me almost mockingly, then clicked.

Vermeer's *Girl with a Pearl Earring* replaced the portrait of the mangled woman. "Now, that's better, isn't it?" he said, using his most seductive tone. The audience relaxed, and Verhaast began to expand on the woman's virginal beauty, her innocence, and yet her intimacy with the viewer. The audience was back on familiar footing once again, and they relaxed into Verhaast's narrative.

Then he paused, stared at me, and clicked. The portrait of the mangled woman appeared again, and the audience held its collective breath.

Somebody called, "Oops, wrong slide!" The audience laughed, though hesitantly.

"Not this time," said Verhaast, and the hall fell silent, waiting for him to explain.

He stared at me but said nothing, letting the horror sink in. With a click, van der Poel's painting returned. The image of ruined Delft was no less harrowing than the portrait of the woman, but not nearly as repulsive. Another click, and the deformed woman appeared side by side with the van der Poel, all without a word from the lectern. A further click, and a grid of four slides filled the screen. At the top, side by side, were Vermeer's *A View of Delft* and *Girl with a Pearl Earring*. At the bottom, side by side, were the van der Poel and the painting of the grotesquely deformed woman. There was no word of explanation; Verhaast let the audience digest the delightful works on top and the horrific at the bottom.

He clicked again, and I blinked rapidly, surprised at what I saw.

A familiar detail from the Carruthers' Fabritius filled the screen. Then Verhaast zoomed outward, projecting the whole painting, including the frame, and finally broke the silence. "This painting came without a title or a signature, so I called it *The Studio*," he began. "It's been called a

Fabritius. Some scholars were initially of the opinion that it was a Vermeer, but I suspect that it might be neither, merely the work of one of the masters' more talented pupils."

I hoped Verhaast couldn't see my expression in the darkened auditorium. At Thanksgiving two years before, while giving his impromptu cocktail-hour lecture about the Carruthers' Fabritius, he had suggested that it might actually be a Vermeer, pleasing Danielle's father to no end. The man was obviously a liar, but which conclusion was the truth?

Was either? And what did this have to do with Vermeer's women?

Verhaast glanced at the screen behind him, then added with a wink to the packed gallery, "I'd give half my kingdom to know who this talented pupil was. A pity he didn't sign his canvas." He folded his arms, then looked back out at the audience, picking me out of the shadows. "If I had to guess, though, I'd say the person who painted this work was also the artist who painted *this*."

A click brought the grotesque woman back to the screen, and Verhaast grinned. "Yes, the one you all seem to love so much."

The audience stirred in satisfaction as if they had just glimpsed into the mind of a great man, but I felt Verhaast's performance was a private note to me. I just wished I knew what the hell he wasn't telling me.

The audience, as usual, gave Verhaast a standing ovation, and I stood so as not to be conspicuous. In the questions that followed, a woman in the third row asked, "Given that the aesthetic of a painting is established, what difference does it make whether it's a Vermeer or a Fabritius?"

Verhaast chuckled smugly. "About twenty million dollars, to be conservative," he replied—a very un-Professor Verhaast answer.

The crowd laughed—surely the great art historian didn't mean to put a dollar sign on art. A follow-up question came from a woman in the fifth row: "So what would be the difference if the same painting, still retaining its high aesthetic value, was found to be by this unknown pupil?"

"Fifty million," said Verhaast with a vaudevillian straight face. "And the collapse of the art market and Western civilization as we know it."

The crowd laughed, relieved that he wasn't serious.

"We have time for one last question," Verhaast said, staring at the projection booth or at me. Then, he pointed at a female student in the middle of the hall. She asked about the sunlight breaking through the heavy clouds in Vermeer's *View of Delft*. It was clearly a planted question, letting Verhaast end his lecture with brilliance and flourish, and he took full advantage of the setup.

I HADN'T PLANNED TO STICK around. My goal that day was to hear the lecture and get out, grab an early dinner in the dining hall, and keep my meeting with Josh, who needed to pass his statistics course to graduate. Josh was many things—my friend, my occasional hook-up, my purveyor of vegan oatmeal cookies (surprisingly good, and now my vice)—but he was never going to be a mathematician. I gathered my things and stayed in my seat as the applause waned, waiting for Verhaast and his entourage to leave the stage, when to my horror he stopped at the wing, turned to the back of the hall, and called, "Sabrina, would you join us in my office for a minute?"

My stomach flopped. It hadn't been my imagination, after all—Verhaast knew damn well I was there and he had revised his lecture because I was there. I wanted to run back to the safety of my dorm room, but I forced myself to stand and give him a little salute of acknowledgement.

Danielle was at stake.

Of course, I realized that going back to Verhaast's office would wreck me for the rest of the day. Feeling guilty, I sent Josh a quick text that something had come up and we'd have to do his problem set the next evening, then made my way through the crowd and crossed the street through a biting rain to Verhaast's office.

The department secretary showed me in without hesitation—what was one more bedraggled student during finals, anyway?—and I found Verhaast waiting with his people, who stood around the walls of his large office as if the furniture were off-limits.

The camel-colored leather couch was still there, and I didn't close the door.

"Would you please give us a minute?" Verhaast asked the room, and his entourage began to file past me into the waiting room. "You too, Veronica," he said, addressing a tall, voluptuous woman who hesitated next to the desk. She looked at me as if I were the new *it* about to take her place in Verhaast's bed. "Don't go far. This'll be quick," he said, giving her his most reassuring smile. "Oh, and close the door behind you, wouldn't you?"

When the latch clicked, he turned to me without preliminaries or niceties and said, "You disappoint me, Sabrina. I expected you to ask about Hanna Deursen."

I saw the trap and shrugged the way I had shrugged for the two detectives when I evaded their questions. "Who's Hanna Deursen?" I asked.

He stared at me for a long moment. I saw in his eyes the

ebbing disdain art historians reserve for those who forget details. Even in my brief time in his class, I'd had Verhaast's mantra drilled into me: *Details. Details. Details. The heart and soul of art history. And the total recall of these details at the right time.* And yet, here I was, a Yale senior—in his eyes, I was sure, an undeserving Yale student—who forgot her lesson. I could feel his displeasure—and who was I to have failed him? A Colombian charity case, good for pizza delivery at the most, a piece of flesh taken and tossed aside.

It took all of my resolve, but I kept my expression blank and didn't flinch.

The madness that the name of Hanna Deursen had sparked in Danielle's eyes when Verhaast had mentioned it at Thanksgiving was now in his eyes. "Should I know her?" I added, employing the same innocent shrug.

His eyes narrowed. "Did Danielle ever mention Deursen to you?"

I made a face. "No, I don't think so...wait, is that her cousin from West Virginia? No, that's Donahue..."

The act worked, and he gave up on me.

"I'm sorry about Danielle," he said, breaking into small talk as his shoulders relaxed. "I'd give half my kingdom to find her."

"Is that all, Professor?"

He dismissed me. I was useless to him.

I glanced at Veronica and the others in the hall as I let myself out. "He's all yours, kids," I said, shouldering my pack, and made my way out into the rain.

At that moment, I would have given half my kingdom to unlock Danielle's Hanna Deursen file.

TWO WEEKS AFTER DANIELLE DISAPPEARED, JUST AS HOPE WAS
fading that she'd met someone exciting and run off on
a fling, my dean called me into his office for a private
chat. When I'd made myself comfortable on his vinyl couch,
he came around his desk and sat beside me, then took my
hand and quietly explained the provision in the students'
bylaws helping roommates cope with tragedy.

"I know this has been hard on you, Sabrina," he said,
giving my hand a little squeeze. "And I don't want this
to affect your academic record. If you need to drop your
classes this term, go ahead—it won't hurt your GPA or your
transcript."

I nodded, trying to stay stoic, but a few tears leaked out,
and I tried to sniff them back
into place.

He reached behind
him to the end table and
plucked up a Kleenex box,
which he pressed into my
free hand without a word.
I released his grip and
hugged the box as if it
were a connection to
my missing roommate,

not bothering to wipe my tears. After a while—I hoped it was a short while—I dried my eyes and blew my nose, and he patted my shoulder.

"I went over your records, Sabrina," my dean continued, and opened a folder to reveal my transcript. "You're in a good shape. Distributional requirements finished, language requirement met—German?" He seemed genuinely surprised. "Interesting. Why German?"

"It was the only language class I could fit into my schedule," I admitted, balling the tissue in my fist. "Well, the only language class that didn't require me to learn a new alphabet. Advanced Spanish conflicted with other classes, so German it was."

"Do you speak Spanish, then?"

"Rudimentary. My mother does, and I've wanted to read *Don Quixote* in the original since high school. Still working on that."

"And how's your German?" he asked.

"Well, I passed," I answered with a smile, my first since I walked into his office.

I didn't tell him that I fell in love with the language, and that Danielle and I spent the summer between our sophomore and junior years in Germany. She roamed the museums, and I enrolled in the Berlin School of Languages on a summer grant. We returned home, Danielle with her head full of European masterpieces, and I with proficiency in German.

"Look, Sabrina," my dean said, putting the folder down, "you already have the credits you need to graduate. Your GPA is impressive. You don't have to struggle—"

"It's okay, Dean B. I'll manage," I whispered.

I didn't want to be idle, floating like a zombie around

campus waiting for graduation or, I prayed, for Danielle
to reappear. In fact, I argued, going to class and doing the
work would help me take my mind off Danielle.

He had doubts, but I prevailed.

Of course, I didn't tell him that even with a full course
load, I didn't take my mind off Danielle and Verhaast for
a second.

In the wee hours, when sleep eluded me and my thoughts
turned to Danielle, I cried to myself in my lonely room and
hoped she was safe, wherever she was. But then I forced
myself to think of Verhaast, the smug bastard, and dry my
eyes. My conviction that he was involved in Danielle's disappearance never faltered, even as the police kept prodding
me for answers I couldn't give.

As September chilled into October, I tried to keep going
to class, but I couldn't concentrate on the reading. Falling
behind and useless in discussion, I started to cut, though I
didn't yet inform my dean of my problems.

I joined my classmates in the dining hall, but my heavy
silence made some of them uncomfortable, and so I walked
through the maze of basement corridors that connected my
residential college to the one next door and took my meals
over there, alone and in relative anonymity. People stared,
but they gave me my space.

I helped Josh with his stats, but he couldn't understand
why I'd lost my appetite for him. I liked Josh—among his
other qualities, he was a gentle lover, surprisingly skilled
and willing to take suggestions—but my mind was far away,
and our last attempt that season ended in failure, with me
curled on the edge of the skinny bed, clutching my knees,

and Josh spooning reassuringly behind me. "They're going to find her," he whispered. "Sabrina, you can't keep blaming yourself. Talk to me, okay?"

I didn't say a word, but I turned to his chest and cried in his arms.

JOSH NEVER GAVE UP ON Danielle and never doubted me. Still, I couldn't trust him with my research—I didn't know what he would think if he knew I'd kept Danielle's computer and files—and so, the afternoon after Verhaast's last public lecture of the semester, I made up a vague excuse to get out of stats practice, locked myself in my room, turned off my phone, and skipped dinner. I needed to concentrate, and with a box of Ritz crackers at my side, I moved my computer's components to the floor, opened Danielle's laptop in its place, and got to work.

Something about the grid Verhaast had used in his lecture spoke to me, and I created a six squares grid, three-by-two. Instead of paintings, I filled the squares with names: Rembrandt, Fabritius, Vermeer on top, Verhaast, Danielle, Hanna Deursen below. I stared at my work, hoping some connection would pop out at me, and when lightning failed to strike, I added a seventh square to the bottom of the grid and wrote, "the mangled woman." Momentarily satisfied, I printed the grid and pinned it to the corkboard above my desk.

I needed space, and so I took Danielle's paper file to the common room and spread its contents out on the wooden floor, hoping for a clue. The password for the locked Hanna Deursen file *had* to be there—Danielle would have written it down, surely!—but the paper mosaic turned up no new secrets.

Only one document continued to puzzle me in that

it was so unlike the rest of Danielle's notes: an inventory of the objects in the thirty-five known Vermeer paintings. Pearls, letters, jackets, musical instruments, maps, wine, jugs, draperies—every single object was noted, tallied, and cross-referenced against other paintings. I had no idea what Danielle had been hoping to uncover—sometimes, I reasoned, a pearl earring is just a pearl earring, nothing more—and so I reluctantly put the inventory away and resumed my search for the enigmatic password.

It was well after midnight when I packed the papers away again and listened to my messages. Josh had left several, claiming he was in desperate need of my help, that this was the last set of the semester, and that he was going to fail out and have to work at an Applebee's in Iowa for the rest of his life if I didn't help the numbers make sense. Linda, my neighbor, had called to check on me since she hadn't seen me at dinner. She hoped I had finally hooked up with somebody and wished me luck. My mother had also left a message, sounding tired and worried. She always panicked when a letter from the bursar arrived, and twice a year, like clockwork, I had to explain to her that my tuition was still paid and she wasn't on the hook for more money than she'd make that year. At that moment, I loved her very much, and I made a mental note to call her at a decent hour.

Having gotten nowhere in my work, and slightly giddy with the hour, I called Josh. His groggy greeting told me I'd woken him. "Hey, you. If you're not drunk, meet me at the library."

"Sabrina," he muttered, "for God's sake, it's one o'clock in the morning."

"So bring your sleepy ass to the library."

"Come here. Leon's out tonight—"

"Josh," I cut him off, "I want to talk to you."

He paused as the tone of my voice cut through his mental fog. "Oh shit, you're not pregnant, are you?"

"See you at the library," I said, and hung up.

There was no need to specify a location—only one library was open at that hour of the night, and half of the patrons remaining would be asleep over their books, waiting for security to kick them out. I brushed my hair, shoved on a hat and gloves, then grabbed Danielle's laptop and trekked through the sleet to the underground entrance.

Five minutes after I chose a table and texted Josh my coordinates, he showed up, sleep-mussed and still wearing Tabasco-print pajama pants over flip-flops. "Okay," he whispered, slipping into the chair across the table from me, "what the heck is going on?"

"I'm not pregnant, so breathe," I replied, then pushed the laptop toward him. The desktop was innocuous enough, and as a precaution, I'd renamed the Hanna Deursen file, "Notes." "Working on my thesis, locked the file for security, forgot the password. Can you help me?"

Josh squinted at the screen and rubbed his face. "The hell, Sabrina," he muttered. "What's so damn important that it needs security?"

"I've got data from a dozen telescopes on there," I lied, reaching over the screen to tap the renamed folder. "My calculations. You know how long it takes to compile that crap? I didn't want some dumb cop going through my computer and messing it up by accident."

He shook his head. "It's called a backup copy. Make one next time." With that, he passed the laptop to me and shrugged. "Sorry, but you're asking the wrong guy. Try Marco or Jamal, but wait for sunrise, huh?"

"Josh," I began as he pushed back from the table, but he raised his hands to stop me.

"Library's about to close, I'm tired, and I've got class at eight-fucking-thirty," he said, and shoved his hood up. *"Goodnight*, Sabrina."

I waited, watching until the elevator door closed behind him, then stared at the computer before me. Even with its new name, the Hanna Deursen file seemed to mock me...

And I needed to get a grip.

The security guard tapped his wrist, and I slipped my outerwear back on. The night was young.

REALISTICALLY, I SHOULDN'T HAVE BEEN annoyed by Josh's reaction, but it was close to two a.m. by the time I locked my door, and few wise decisions are ever made at that hour. Frustrated and unreasonably peeved, I pulled out my milk crate of clippings, spread the contents across the floor, and knelt beside my mess. I hadn't touched the crate in nearly a year, but that night seemed as good a time as any to revisit Verhaast's work.

His seminal paper on Vermeer's women—titled, appropriately enough, "Vermeer's Women"—was among the many publications in my crate, and had been one of the first items I filed away. This paper, in a slightly different form, had morphed into a chapter in one of Verhaast's books; it was part of any anthology that dealt with seventeenth-century paintings and the history of art, and was widely quoted. When I read the paper for the first time, I highlighted its opening sentence: "We know very little about Vermeer's women." Then, out of sheer curiosity, which I couldn't explain now and most likely couldn't have explained then, I highlighted the names of the women Verhaast mentioned. On the long list of references at the end of the paper, I highlighted the sources referring to the names.

I hadn't expected to find anything revelatory in that paper, but when I flipped it over to return it to the crate, I noticed a new list of names handwritten at the end of the references and pulled it closer for a fresh look.

Danielle was the only person who knew about my obsession with going after Verhaast. She had dissuaded me from trying to use his foreign accounts against him, claiming it was petty, and in general, she tried to persuade me to let it go. "He's been at this for at least forty years," she said one afternoon as I filed new papers into my crate. "He knows *everyone* in the field, Sabrina. Just drop it."

I continued to work, ignoring her.

"Listen to me," Danielle pleaded, grabbing my wrist. "It's not worth it. He could hurt you, okay?"

I didn't look up. "He already has."

Danielle let me nurse the milk crate with the hope that I, too, would eventually see the futility of revenge. But I didn't expect that she would use my own clippings to communicate with me.

In her perfect handwriting, Danielle had written, "Hanna Deursen," who wasn't mentioned in the paper as one of Vermeer's women—or, for that matter, in any published article that I'd seen. As far as I knew, Deursen had never existed in the literature, and yet Danielle had a locked file about her on the laptop. Under Deursen's name, Danielle had written, "Didrika Margrit Aken," the name of the Irish woman who had vanished, and under that, she'd written a male name I hadn't seen before, "Fredrick William Krinsky."

Below Krinsky's name, Danielle had drawn a line, under which she wrote, "ME."

I stared at the list for a long, silent moment. Was the ME referring to Danielle, or was she warning me? And if so, about what?

The last bit of writing was a date below "ME"—three days before Danielle vanished.

I TURNED TO GOOGLE.

A search of Aken's name yielded the same Irish newspaper clippings I had already filed away. Hanna Deursen's name drew a blank. But Fredrick William Krinsky had hits aplenty.

Krinsky had been the curator and the manager of a small museum in a village tucked on a gentle hillside in the northeast of Belgium, near the borders of Germany and Holland. The village—Het Klooster Stad, "the Convent Village"—barely warranted a dot on the map, but several of Danielle's documents explained the village's provenance. On top of the hill was an ancient convent, the Convent of the Blessed Virgin, and the museum Krinsky oversaw preserved the convent's history and sold artifacts connected to or inspired by the nuns cloistered there. My Dutch and French were nonexistent, but I eventually found a German blurb online discussing Krinsky's disappearance and asking the public for information. The picture accompanying the article showed the feeble seventy-eight-year-old man who had apparently vanished without a trace.

Danielle had given me three names of people who had disappeared. Hanna Deursen and Didrika Aken had connections to Verhaast. I didn't know enough about Fredrick

Krinsky to make that call yet, but my instinct suggested I'd find a link soon enough, especially since Danielle had taken the time to make copious notes about a place seemingly unrelated to the rest of her research. I pulled the Het Klooster Stad documents from the pile and set them aside, knowing with sick certainty that they were important somehow. As far as I could deduce, Danielle was either instructing me to look up Fredrick William Krinsky or directing me to the Convent of the Blessed Virgin.

Mulling this question over, I poked around online until I found a reference to Didrika Aken's sister in Sligo and a phone number. By four a.m., I figured I could make the call without incurring unnecessary transatlantic wrath.

Didrika's sister had been puzzled when I introduced myself, but once I mentioned that I was an art history student, her tone softened. "I saw Ms. Aken's name in a few footnotes," I explained, "and I'd hoped to talk to her for my senior thesis. I, uh...I heard she'd gone missing."

The lady on the other end—Marta, she insisted I call her—was as helpful as she could be, but she had nothing new to offer as to her sister's whereabouts. She asked me a few questions about my studies, and I lied as well as I could, falling back on snippets remembered from Danielle's conversations—and occasionally quoting Verhaast, of all people.

After a few minutes, I casually asked if her sister had spent any time in Belgium. "Oh my, yes," Marta said, and I could hear the smile in her voice. "She went many times. You know, I still have postcards she sent from this little village, Het Klooster Stad. Gorgeous scenery. Dear Didrika loved the place and especially the Convent of the Blessed Virgin there. She was very devout, you know. "

Five minutes later, I brought our conversation to a polite

end and stared out my window at the upper courtyard of our college, waiting for the sun to rise.

That was it. Danielle was telling me—almost ordering me—to visit the Convent of the Blessed Virgin in Belgium.

I INFORMED MY DEAN THAT I'd take him up on his offer to cut my classes next semester. Travel, I told him, would help me get over Danielle's disappearance. He allowed me to use the college prize money I had received earlier in the year. "Maybe Latin America," I told him, which was also the story I spread among my friends. I dropped hints about looking up cousins in Colombia and making the trek to Machu Picchu, the better to give my plans substance among them.

Sure, it would have been nice if someone had known I'd be in Belgium, but my gut warned me that I'd be safer if neither Verhaast nor the police knew where I'd gone.

I FELT I NEEDED TO MAKE ONE STOP BEFORE LEAVING FOR BELGIUM. I met Danielle's mother in person only once after the police classified Danielle as missing. We'd spoken on the phone several times, but I couldn't bring myself to go to the Carruthers' house, and neither of them seemed keen on coming yet again to New Haven. Two days before leaving the country, I called Westport and asked for a meeting. Josh loaned me his car for the day. He'd offered to drive me, but I insisted on going alone, not knowing what I'd say or how I'd react when I faced Mrs. Carruthers.

She had been polite as ever on the phone when I made the arrangements, but all the warmth I'd remembered was gone from the house when I stepped into the foyer.

There was something heavy and unspeakably sad in the air. Mrs. Carruthers stood by the staircase in silence, still perfectly coiffed but looking somehow as if she'd been stretched thin. Her grief was audible even as she welcomed me and wrapped me in a tight hug, and I tried not to cry.

I knew she was too kind to wonder why her pale, perfect Danielle had gone missing instead of me, the chubby Latina in her arms—at least, too kind to express such sentiments aloud—but still, I couldn't shake the feeling that I represented the loss.

We spoke our banalities, and then I blurted out, "Look, I'm from Chicago. No one's really gone until we find the body."

She looked at me in silence, and for once, I couldn't tell whether she agreed or thought I was a complete idiot.

She didn't walk me to the door.

The trip back to campus had been miserable. I sobbed all the way to New Haven, and when my tears showed no signs of slowing, I stopped at a gas station on I-95 and bought cheap sunglasses to cover my red eyes. Still, I couldn't fool Josh, who brought me dinner from the dining hall and stayed the night. I cried in his arms and secretly was thankful that he didn't move to make love.

Josh dozed off around ten with his arms around me, and I listened to his easy, steady breathing, free of worry and pain, the carefree sleep of a privileged guy from the Upper East Side. Sweet Josh. At that moment, for the first time, I thought I might love him.

I stirred on my back, careful not to wake him, and stared at the ceiling in the dark room, lost in thought. The meeting with Danielle's mother reeled in my head in beats and reflections, like a ball bouncing from pin to pin, in search of a nuance, a clue...when it hit me with a start.

The Carruthers' Fabritius, that chaotic glimpse into the

artist's studio, contained all the objects on Danielle's weird inventory.

I had been so careful not to offend Danielle's mother, not to cry, not to blurt out, "I know who abducted your daughter," that I failed to think of the painting—just as I had failed to connect the inventory with the painting when I first dug through Danielle's file. It was suddenly so clear to me, and I sat up on the edge of the bed, holding my head.

Josh stirred beside me, roused by my movement, and rubbed my bare shoulder. "Sabrina, babe, you've got to relax. There's nothing you can do, not tonight." He pushed himself upright and wrapped his arms around me, pulling me against him. "What happened? Bad dream?"

"It's nothing," I muttered, and let him guide me back to the thin mattress.

We made love in the morning like it was our last time together, and then Josh slipped off for class, decently rested if still wearing the previous day's clothes. When I was alone, I fished Danielle's inventory of Vermeer's paintings out of its folder and studied it carefully. She had labeled it "The Objects in Vermeer's Paintings"; she could just as easily have labeled it "The Objects in Fabritius's Painting in My Parents' House."

And then, after breakfast, I reread the file she had labeled "The Convent of the Blessed Virgin."

I WAS RAISED A GOOD Catholic, so I grew up with the tales of the miraculous, strange, and just plain gross deeds attributed to the saints. "Mortification of the flesh" was a term that entered my vocabulary at a tender age to explain why these holy, supposedly good people were always starving and whipping themselves. My teachers explained the purpose of mortification in various ways—penance, sacrifice, atonement, unity with the Son in His suffering—but even the best scriptural rationale for the practice did nothing to make *Lives of the Saints* look less like a horror novel. Still, even as numb as I'd become to the gristlier side of the faith, I found the accounts of the Convent of the Blessed Virgin stomach-turning.

The origins of the Convent of the Blessed Virgin were murky, but the place was long established by the tenth century, when a young woman from a well-to-do family turned up on their doorstep. Her parents had betrothed her against her will to a godless older man, and the poor girl was looking for an escape. The Sisters took her in and shielded her when her intended's men came to claim her, but the men wouldn't be turned away so easily. Hearing the struggle in the halls, the girl fled to the chapel, where, by some miracle, she found a golden knife laying on the altar. Praying to the Virgin Mother for protection, she took up the blade and began slashing at herself, leaving her face a ruined mess by the time the men found her. The old man quickly broke off the engagement, and the disfigured girl was free to remain cloistered within the convent, blinded and scarred but secure in her virginity.

Seeing the girl's miraculous salvation, or perhaps motivated to escape their own matrimonial situations, other newcomers to the convent followed her gruesome example. At some point, the Church tried to put a stop to the practice, but old habits die hard, and no one in Rome cared much about a tiny convent in the middle of nowhere. Rumors persisted of extreme mortification: nuns who cut their faces, extracted their teeth, burned their breasts, and mutilated their nipples out of piety. A few gouged out their eyes, letting infection fester in the wounds, further deforming their bodies in order to remove any lustful possibilities. "Looking at the pictures, I don't think virginity is a difficult status to maintain for the most devoted," Danielle had remarked in her notes.

I could almost hear the snide edge to her voice as I read her neat handwriting. Danielle, the archetypical WASP, hadn't grown up with a Church-sanctioned compendium of horror stories, and she often turned to me for an explanation when a painting's symbolism was too obscure. I could tell she believed few of the stories—Methodism was a fairly straightforward, no-frills version of the faith, as far as I could see, and allowed little room for, say, bilocating holy men—and she often dismissed my tales with a raised eyebrow and a muttered, "Uh-huh, *right.*" Yet, she researched and recorded the story of the miller's daughter.

The accounts in Danielle's file varied in their details, but the gist was the same. In 1536, give or take a decade, a deformed girl was born to a poor miller on the outskirt of Delft. His wife died in childbirth, and his neighbors assumed the baby was demonic. Fearing the child's supposed powers, they tried to force him to hand her over to be burned alive. But the miller took pity on his infant daughter and feared for his own life, so he wrapped the baby up in a sack and sneaked out the back door. After seven days and nights of trudging across the countryside, he arrived at the Convent of the Blessed Virgin, the only place on earth he knew would take care of a deformed infant, and entrusted the baby to the Mother Superior.

The miller returned to his village empty-handed, where he found his house and mill a mess of burned rubble, his wife's body nothing more than ashes. Devastated, he kept walking to Rotterdam, then hired himself out on a ship sailing to the Far East. Ten years later, he returned to Delft a wealthy man, and he made the trip to visit his daughter, who was beautiful in spirit but still as hideous as the nuns who'd raised her. Mother Superior had named her Helen, as she had come into their care on the feast day of St. Helena the empress. The former miller left the nuns with a sizeable contribution and named his first ship in his daughter's honor.

It was another five years before he visited Het Klooster Stad again, and he returned even wealthier, the owner of a fleet of ships and warehouses in Rotterdam and Amsterdam. Helen was now a young woman, aware of her deformities but beautiful in her devotion to the Lord. From then on, her father made his visits more regular, though he still spent months on the coast, managing his fortune, which he was happy to share with the Sisters.

When word finally circulated in Delft of the former miller's good luck, his once-neighbors sought him out, ostensibly to seek his forgiveness but more practically to ask for loans. Someone realized that his infrequent visits to the convent always occurred near the feast day of St. Helena, and gradually, the destitute began to make the trip ahead of him, hoping to partake in his largesse when he visited his daughter. The little village of Het Klooster Stad was hardly large enough to accommodate the growing numbers of pilgrims, and so the veiled Sisters took it upon themselves to see to the travelers' welfare, offering them food for a minimal contribution and wine for a little more. Within a few years, the annual pilgrimage became a lucrative event for the town and convent alike. The faithful camped outside the walls of the convent, praying for the miller's health, lighting candles in memory of his wife, and raving about the beauty of his daughter—for a legend had sprung up that the deformed child miraculously grew into a beautiful woman.

With the additional revenue, the nuns had a chapel constructed outside the convent walls to meet the pilgrims' spiritual needs. A local artist painted a glorious altarpiece of the Madonna and Child, using all of his considerable skill to render the Virgin's face angelic in its beauty. The pilgrims whispered that he had surely used the fair Helen as his model. When the chapel was completed, the Mother Superior assigned nuns to pray for the health of the afflicted, asking fees proportional to the number of prayers. Painters sold copies of the altarpiece, and soon they painted their own versions of the miller's daughter, swearing she had posed for them in their dreams.

There's no official account of what became of Helen herself, but it's safe to say her face launched a lucrative event for the little convent. Through the years, thousands of the deformed and afflicted journeyed to Het Klooster Stad and prayed in the chapel with the hope that God would hear and bestow on them the same miracle He had performed for the miller's daughter. Of course, Rome eventually got word and intervened. "A few moved for the beatification of Helen," Danielle noted at the bottom of one printout, "but nothing came of it. The Vatican put a stop to the pilgrimage, and the village largely dried up. Still, it appears that a few desperate souls continue to traveled to Het Klooster Stad in search of a miracle to this day—copies of the altarpiece are available in the gift shop," Danielle had written, and neatly added a URL.

She had also printed two pictures side by side and stapled them to the back of the article. Vermeer's famous painting

Girl with a Pearl Earring next to a painting unknown to me of Mary with the infant Jesus. I thought little of it until I visited the site Danielle had written down and realized that the painting I was seeing was the chapel's altarpiece, and that the faces of the Virgin and Vermeer's anonymous girl bore a strangely similar quality, superficially distinct but alike in grace. "The face of the miller's daughter in these paintings is as angelic and virginal as those of Vermeer's women," Daniel had noted in the margin.

As I reread Danielle's notes, the broad contours of an idea began to take shape, but the details remained elusive. Still, I knew two things. First, there was something deeply wrong with the disappearance of Het Klooster Stad's museum's curator, an elderly man who looked like the kind of guy who'd gently shoo flies out open windows. Secondly, although I couldn't yet prove it, something convinced me that the picture of the mangled woman Verhaast had shown in his lecture was actually a portrait of a nun. And both, I felt in my gut, were connected to Verhaast and Danielle's disappearance.

The evening before I left campus, I told Josh I might be heading for Spain. He had lent me his backpack for the trip, as I didn't want to travel with the expensive leather backpack Danielle's mother had given me three Christmases before, and came by to help me with my final preparations. "Linguistic immersion without worrying about water quality," I joked, making light of our parting. "Might even hop across to Morocco. It's not far, you know."

"I wish I could go with you," he said, lacing his fingers

through mine as we stood together in the wreckage of my common room. "You'll take pictures, right?"

"Definitely."

"And put them up on Facebook?"

"You've got it," I lied, letting him pull me into his arms. "The better to make you all insanely jealous of my awesome life."

He held me for a long moment, and as I listened to his heartbeat through his soft sweatshirt, I wanted to hold on forever.

It was Josh who broke away first, but only to reach for his back pocket and extract his battered leather wallet. "Here, I want you to take this," he said in a rush, pulling a black Visa card free and pressing it into my hand. "Just in case you find a souvenir I'd like," he added, laughing to cover his embarrassment.

"Josh," I protested, "I can't—"

"Yes, you can. Just in case of an emergency, to ensure you'll come back for graduation."

"I have a roundtrip ticket," I pointed out.

"Sabrina," he insisted, "take it. You know what I mean."

I did, and I put it into my purse as he watched, but I resolved not to pull it out again. As little as I wanted to give the authorities a paper trail to trace me to the Belgian backwoods, I also didn't want to have to explain to Josh why he was getting bills from somewhere far beyond the parameters of the Spanish vacation I'd told him about.

Maybe it was just my paranoia talking, but something told me that Josh would be safer if he could honestly tell Verhaast that he didn't know where I'd gone.

I CALLED MY MOTHER FROM the airport, explaining to her that

the trip to Australia was part of a research class I was enrolled in. Lying to my mother was one of the hardest things I'd ever done, but it was necessary. It would be careless to underestimate Verhaast. "Call me when you get to Sydney," she said in Spanish. I promised and reassured her that I'd return before Commencement. The poor woman had been saving money for the trip for two years. I had already reserved a room for her in one of the finest hotels to let her feel like a queen on the day her only daughter graduated from Yale, and we had accepted the Carruthers' invitation to dinner on Commencement Weekend, but all of that would have to change.

Unless, of course, I found Danielle.

I SPENT TWO HOURS IN THE MUSEUM STORE. HELEN'S FACE WAS everywhere, in all sizes and forms, on painted crosses, plates and tea settings, t-shirts and sweaters, key chains and scarves. There was no depiction of the deformed nuns living up at the end of the road, however, and to my disappointment, nor was there a memorial plaque for Krinsky, who had directed, managed, and curated the little museum for decades.

Two veiled Sisters ran the cash register, each sporting a habit more closely resembling a burka than the modest Carmelite habits with which I was familiar. All was covered but the eyes, revealing nothing of the woman underneath. I could only imagine the deformities and the scars under the habits, and quickly averted my eyes and thoughts. I wanted to ask them if they knew of Krinsky's whereabouts, but the question seemed risky to me, and besides, I had no idea if either spoke English—I

couldn't very well try in German, not with the two German tourists behind me.

They scared me.

They had wandered into the museum store soon after me. I would have ignored them, had I not seen them several times before. They could be easily dismissed—two men in their mid-thirties, stocky and nondescript, like a million other German tourists—but I didn't ignore them.

I was on guard.

They spoke German, and I gave no sign that I understood every word. They tested me. They discussed the chubby Latina with the hot ass and the things they'd like to do to her, which kept drifting back to things only possible with multiple partners. I didn't even glance in their direction. Then, as if to reassure their own conclusion that I didn't know German, the taller of the two said, "Should we tell her about the tear in her skirt?" I kept my attention trained on the picture album telling the history of the convent to resist the urge to check for a rip.

The nuns and I conducted our business by signs and the universally understood passing of a credit card, and I emerged in possession of a decal of what appeared to be the three-masted *Helen*, which bore the now-familiar face on the prow's figurehead. The sticker went on Danielle's laptop for luck, and I hurried off toward my hostel in search of a bite.

But try as I did to shake them, the two Germans almost always happened to be within earshot.

There was no food to be had at the hostel itself—its cafeteria was closed, and the management seemed generally apathetic to its guests needs—but I'd managed to secure a private room for very little, which, in light of the town's usual visitors, came equipped with a handicapped bathroom and slightly rusty handrails. Other than that, the place was damp and smelled musty, and so I decided to make it up to myself by foregoing grocery shopping at the store across the street in favor of taking my meals at the four-star inn at the corner of the cobblestone plaza. The restaurant boasted a veranda with a breathtaking view of the countryside, which was, unfortunately, reflected in the price of the food.

As I enjoyed the sunset, the two German tourists wandered onto the veranda and took a table near mine. They discussed the lovely evening and the weather, but I knew better.

They were just behind me when I inquired at the inn's reception about the chapel at the convent and how to get there.

The next morning, I bypassed both the sad hostel offerings and the expensive Continental buffet at the inn in favor of a quick bite at the coffee shop down the street. The pale winter sun was just peeking over the horizon when I wandered into the warmth of the deserted coffee shop. The jangling bell that had announced my arrival quickly brought a veiled figure out from the back. I ordered my breakfast in rapid German, and I had just pulled out my credit card when the door chimed again and the German duo walked in, rubbing their hands against the chill. Cursing my carelessness, I thanked the nun loudly in English. A second nun appeared behind the counter; unlike her sisters at the museum, this one was visibly hunchbacked, but her gestures seemed welcoming enough as she beckoned me toward the register.

Suspecting that the men would follow me to the chapel, I made a full production of leaving my knapsack with the hunchbacked nun. "I plan to visit the chapel, and this is too heavy," I said to the nun when the two Germans approached to pay for their breakfast. All I wanted was to leave footprints of my whereabouts in the event that I, too, represented a threat.

"Make sure to visit the cemetery," the hunchbacked nun mumbled in German.

I hesitated, trying not to give myself away, then asked her, "Do you speak English?"

She shrugged with whatever shoulder she had under the heavy habit, took my knapsack, and disappeared behind the swinging doors to the kitchen, but the fat nun nodded and replied, "I know a little English."

I acted relieved. "Great, would you please tell me what she just said?"

She translated, and I made a point to mangle the pronunciation of *"danke schon"* as the two Germans laughed gently.

I took the first tram up to the chapel. The village Chamber of Commerce had installed electric trams to replace the horses and wagons—and sometimes the backs of peasants—that had shuttled feeble pilgrims up and down the winding road to the convent. I took a seat behind two nuns on their way back to the convent, apparently at the end of their overnight shift in the village. It was impossible to tell whether they had been the ones behind the counter at the museum store or whether one had been the nun who spoke a bit of English. But I paid more attention to the two German tourists who sat behind me.

Almost on cue, the Germans followed me off the tram and into the chapel. I genuflected in the aisle, then took a moment to study the altarpiece before dropping a coin in a box and lighting a candle. The men stood patiently nearby, waiting for me to rise, and I heard one mutter, "Wonder what deformity *she's* praying about, eh?"

On my way out of the chapel, with the two Germans still close by, I stopped to study a small painting of Jesus cleansing the ten lepers. The work was crude, almost primitive—the sores were blotchy, and the proportions and perspective were all wrong. I glanced at the covered Sister standing beside the painting, who held a wooden box with a slit at the top for coins, and asked, "Is this a Vermeer?"

The two Germans laughed to my ignorance, but the tall one answered in perfect English. "If it were, these ladies wouldn't be asking for charity."

WITH THAT, I COULDN'T IGNORE the men any longer and still be polite. We introduced ourselves outside the chapel, and to keep them from finding me at the hostel, I gave my name as Esther. Once the basics were covered, the taller man— Hans—flashed a crooked smile. "My friend and I tried to guess whether you're Mexican or Puerto Rican, but we did not suspect an American," he said.

Trying for nonchalance, I replied, "Why's that?"

"You're too beautiful for an American," he replied, and both laughed again.

The flirtation felt forced somehow, and I couldn't help but wonder if Hans had been tasked with sweet-talking me. "Thank you," I said, hoping I was blushing.

We strolled through the well-tended, if winter-brown, garden along the walls of the convent and reached the ancient cemetery. The only people who ventured that way were either backpackers or able-bodied family members of the afflicted who wanted a moment of solitude without pushing or lifting. There was no construction for wheelchairs there, and the path grew narrower and less tended. I acted like a tourist, snapping pictures and gushing about the scenery. Fortunately, I didn't have to pretend to be awe-struck by the view from the cemetery, and I silently thought of what Danielle might have said, had she been there—probably some cynical comment about the most mangled creatures living in such perfect beauty.

The short German, who had introduced himself as Fritz, couldn't stop taking pictures, and when he asked Hans and me to pose, Hans put his arm around my shoulders and kept it there longer than was appropriate. I tried to ignore his touch and take in the view. The roofs of the village below were barely visible through the fog. Here and there, I could see the narrow road glimmering in the morning sun, and the trams crawling slowly up and down the road like bloated caterpillars, bending and then disappearing beyond folds and thick woods.

The two Germans slipped in and out of English. Satisfied that when it came to German, I was as alert as the buried dead, they exchanged notes of their trip and how to proceed.

Secretly, I congratulated my instinct to hide my where-abouts from Verhaast. I knew who they were but not yet why they were in the village. When they spoke about their mission, they spoke as if they were agents of an interna-tional insurance company, based in Zurich, specializing in art. Hans had arrived to replace Fritz, who had been inves-tigating lost art or insurance fraud for some time now, and was eager to leave. Hans was hopeful that I would stay so that he could spend a night or two with me in bed.

I swallowed hard to contain my excitement at finding a link in the chain: Aken, vanished; Krinsky, vanished; and the common denominator was Verhaast. But as for what exactly the mission of these two Germans was, I didn't as yet have a clue. I decided to play the dumb, fat Latina they most likely expected me to be.

We walked among the gravestones, all carved from local rock. The names on the stones were of women, the dates stretched back centuries, and as we passed down a row, the engravings grew less and less legible and the dates turned into Roman numerals. The uniform simplicity and elegance of the gravestones and the carved names suggested an attempt to recompense and perhaps to even atone for the brutal ugliness underneath.

One gravestone in the middle stood out, as if a cosmic spotlight was directed at it. Its site had been cleaned of weeds recently, the stone washed, and the engraved letters of the name and date traced and cleaned: *Hanna Deursen 1625–1675.*

I paused before the stone and peered down at it, trying to keep my expression neutral. "Wonder what's so special about this one," I murmured.

"What do you mean?" Hans asked.

I pointed to the grave's manicured surface. "Someone took care of this plot, but not its neighbors. Maybe a relative?" I squatted and traced the date with my gloved fingertip, then added, "*Distant* relative, that is. 1675—that's like, what, ten generations, maybe?"

He knelt beside me and tapped Hanna's death date. "Not a good year in the art world. You know Vermeer, the painter? He died that year."

Vaguely, I was conscious that Fritz was taking pictures of us, but whether he was photographing the gravestone or my reaction, I couldn't say.

"Not a good year for anyone, looks like," I said with a shrug, and pointed to the gravestones on either side of us.

"She wasn't the only one to go. What do you think, plague? Cholera? She was only, what, fifty? Poor thing. Plague was a hell of a way to die."

I wasn't sure whether I had managed to control my heartbeat and my breathing and the knot in my stomach—and I knew that if they had noticed, I was in danger.

I knew the fate of Aken and Krinsky—and now Danielle.

T OWARD THE END OF OUR SOPHOMORE YEAR, BEFORE OUR TRIP
to Germany, I gently goaded Danielle to introduce me
to Isidor Mendelssohn.

My off-hours that year were largely spent on the soccer
field—intramural was all I could commit to with my
schedule—or, more recently as my major solidified, hanging
around the observatory, trying to squeeze in time with a
telescope. Danielle, whose academic interests took her to
slightly more glamorous places, had scored a spring internship at the Metropolitan Museum of Art, which took her
to New York twice a week. I didn't know all the details of
how she'd managed to get the position, especially as a sophomore, but Danielle made enough allusions to her family
friend, good old Professor
Verhaast, for me to put the
pieces together.

7

Over dinners, she'd
tell me stories about her
internship—her favorite
paintings, the most eccen-
tric curators, the vigi-
lante docent who made
it his responsibility
to shoo the homeless

away—but often, the conversation would drift back to the man in Gallery 632.

"He's a sweet old fellow, as far as I can see," she said one evening, stirring creamer into her tea. "Harmless, maybe a little nutty. He's just got a thing for *Young Woman with a Water Pitcher*—you know, the Vermeer," she added, seeing my face cloud. "You'd know it if you saw it."

I filed that away, intending to pull out my phone and discreetly look the painting up when Danielle's attention was elsewhere. "So you've got a nut hanging around—"

"I don't know if he's actually *crazy*," she corrected, "just…maybe a little obsessed. Not the weirdest person in the building, not by a long stretch," she said, smiling in the face of my concern. "And don't worry, security is tight around the museum. I'm fine, Sabrina, really. Don't give me that look."

Fine or not, Danielle continued to talk about the old man in the corner, and after a few meals, I was able to draw a portrait out of her.

The head docent said the fellow was a retired teacher named Isidor Mendelssohn, a German Jew and Auschwitz survivor. He always dressed neatly in a jacket and bowtie, but when the gallery was warm, he'd take off his coat and roll up his sleeves, occasionally revealing the faded blue numbers on the inside of his forearm. Isidor had caught Danielle trying not to stare on one such occasion, and when her tour was complete, he took her aside and gently explained the horrors he had seen. She'd bought him a cup of coffee in the cafeteria, and they'd parted that evening, if not as friends, at least as good acquaintances.

Since then, she'd felt more comfortable around the old man, even if his behavior perplexed her. Inevitably as

Young Woman With a Water Pitcher by Johannes Vermeer

Danielle led her tours into Gallery 632, she'd find Isidor standing against the wall, engaging mostly young visitors in conversation about *Young Woman with a Water Pitcher.* No other Vermeer—or, for that matter, any other masterpiece in the room—held his interest. "I think he has a crush on her," Danielle laughed over dessert one night. "You know, if I could swing it, I'd love to get Professor Verhaast up there for an hour to talk to him."

I'd lowered my fork at that but tried not to be rude. "Oh? Why?"

Danielle glanced at my plate, compared the remaining quantities of our pieces of cake, and helped herself to a bite of mine. "Verhaast authenticated the painting in the first place," she said through a mouthful of chocolate. "Well, he headed up the committee that did. Same difference, right?"

Two weeks later, Danielle seemed distressed upon her return, and I led her to the quiet end of an empty table to find the cause. "Professor Verhaast came up to check on me today," she murmured, absently pushing peas around her plate. "Since he got me the internship and all."

"What happened?"

She put her spoon down and stared into the space over my right shoulder. "He went on my tour. I thought I'd introduce him to Isidor, let them chat about the Vermeer, but as soon as we walked in the room, Isidor left."

"Maybe he had somewhere to be," I suggested, but Danielle shook her head.

"No. I saw his face," she said softly. "He started to smile when he saw me—he always does—but then he looked troubled, and I heard Professor Verhaast say something to one of the security guards, and Isidor ran off." She picked up her spoon again and began to poke at her mashed potatoes. "I think he was scared, Sabrina."

"Of *what?*"

"Exactly."

As Danielle continued to pick at her dinner, I knew I had to meet her mysterious friend. At that time, Danielle had no reason to know of my vendetta against Verhaast. My milk crate was well hidden under my bed, and I had yet to tell her what her beloved professor had done to me the year before. I had actually told no one—sexual assault seminars aside, I was humiliated and anxious that my peers and professors would think less of me if the truth came out. More importantly, how was I supposed to look my mother in the face and tell her I'd let a man I'd barely known fuck me? Her disappointment, on top of everything else, would have been too much.

But here was this odd old man in love with *Young Woman with a Water Pitcher* and terrified of Verhaast.

IT WASN'T DIFFICULT TO CONVINCE Danielle to let me come along on one of her tours. I promised not to ask embarrassing questions, and she did her best to pretend she didn't know me for the duration, maintaining an enviable professional façade.

The Met, Danielle had explained on the train, instructed its guides to choose five pieces, each distinct from the others in period, style, culture, and geography, and lecture their tour groups about them as exemplars. On her tour, Danielle started with a Roman urn, moved the group to a South Pacific ritual sculpture, and from there to the American Pavilion and its sculpture of Diana. As usual, I was struck by her vast knowledge of art history and her grace and humor in public. No question was too ridiculous, and Danielle easily shot from the hip. And then, with a little wink for me, she led us toward the Dutch collection.

Gallery 632—Vermeer and His Contemporaries—was a corner room filled with canvasses I recognized from glances through Danielle's textbooks, paintings by Pieter de Hooch and Fabritius and, most prominently, a selection by Vermeer himself. As Danielle shepherded us in, I quickly spotted a hunched, lanky man with nearly white hair, who stood in a corner with his hands clasped. He didn't quite fill out his brown tweed coat, and his green bowtie was a bit loose around his neck, but his dark eyes were warm and smiled at Danielle, and I knew I'd found her Isidor. His gaze met mine briefly, and he nodded a greeting as Danielle began her lecture.

Unsurprisingly, the item Danielle had chosen in this gallery was *Young Woman with a Water Pitcher*. I'd heard many of the details she discussed before, and so I surreptitiously watched Isidor as Danielle spoke, noting the fire in his eyes—a look I thought I recognized from the Thanksgiving before, when Danielle listened to Verhaast mention Hanna Deursen. The group showed its appreciation with applause when Danielle ended her talk. She smiled and nodded her thanks, but before the group could move to the next item— and as Danielle had forewarned me—Isidor's steady voice rose over the percussion: "Danielle, dear, would you please tell us the provenance of that painting?"

"Of course, Mr. Mendelssohn," she replied, craning her neck to meet his eyes over the crowd. "Thank you for reminding me." She cleared her throat, then turned her attention back to the painting and waited until she had the group's attention once more. "It's really fascinating to trace the journeys of these masterpieces—you see all the points at which something could have gone catastrophically wrong, but didn't."

Even I began to pay attention at that.

"As I mentioned," said Danielle, "*Young Woman with a Water Pitcher* was painted between 1600 and 1602, almost certainly in Vermeer's studio in Delft. When it left his hands, it ended up in a tavern next door. By the nineteenth century, it was being passed around to collectors in England, Ireland, and France, and eventually, it wound up in the hands of one Henry Marquand, an American philanthropist and art collector, who paid $800 for the painting around 1888 or 1889." Her audience tittered at the absurdly low sum, and Danielle grinned at their reaction. "Fortunately for all of us here at the Met, Mr. Marquand was a major benefactor of the museum when it was young, and he thought *Young Woman with a Water Pitcher* would be best suited for public display. We're certainly glad he felt that way, and if you wander back to the American Wing and look in Gallery 774, you'll find his portrait on display. But I digress."

I cut my eyes to Isidor, who stood against the wall with an unreadable expression on his face.

"Now," Danielle continued, "as I'm sure you're aware, museums occasionally send parts of their collection on tour, and the Met's no exception. More than two million works of art are housed here—we can certainly afford to loan out a few from time to time." Again, the group chuckled, but Danielle remained solemn. "In fact, we agreed to send *Young Woman with a Water Pitcher* home for a few months in 1935. A restoration team in Amsterdam offered to work on the painting, which by then was showing the usual signs of wear, and so it stayed in Amsterdam for several years. Does anyone here recall what happened to Europe in the late thirties and early forties?"

The laughter that time was knowing and subdued.

"Exactly," she replied. "When the Nazis invaded the Netherlands in 1940, *Young Woman with a Water Pitcher* was among the millions of art objects they looted and shipped off to Germany. There it remained, hanging in Hitler's private gallery, until the liberation. And then it went missing." She looked around the semicircle of visitors, who watched her raptly. "No one knew where it was until 1962, when an anonymous donor returned it to us—no name given, no ransom asked, just a cardboard box addressed to the Director and postmarked in New Jersey, and the Vermeer inside. So, what do you think the Met did next?" she said, smiling once more. When the group shrugged, Danielle grinned more widely. "We cleaned it up and shipped it back to Europe on tour in 1966. *That* time, it visited The Hague and Paris, and then it came home to us in a timely fashion, and aside from a few little excursions in the years since then, it's been hanging here, safe and sound. Is that about right, Mr. Mendelssohn?" she asked, again meeting his eyes over the crowd.

"Close enough," he murmured, and nodded his approval.

Danielle had told me earlier that, without fail, some member of her group would sidle over to Isidor before leaving and ask if he were the anonymous donor. "Not quite," he always said, smiling his enigmatic smile.

DANIELLE GUIDED THE TOUR TO her next stop, the special Matisse exhibit, which was about to close, but I stayed in Gallery 632. As I approached Isidor's corner of the room, he smiled and nodded, then said, "And now, young lady, you want to ask me whether I'm the anonymous donor?"

"Let me guess—not quite," I replied.

Isidor regarded me closely for a moment, then laughed. "Ah, so you're Sabrina, yes? Danielle mentioned you would be here today. Come," he said, linking his arm with mine, "you look famished. Have you been to E.A.T.?"

"I, uh...not since breakfast," I replied, surprised to find myself being guided toward the steps.

"Not *eat*, E.A.T., the café. Sandwiches, soups, caviar, the usual. We'll have plenty of time to talk about the importance of the provenance of *Young Woman with a Water Pitcher*. That is the question on your mind, yes?"

"Absolutely," I replied, wondering how I could politely steer the conversation to Verhaast.

DANIELLE WAS PLEASANTLY SURPRISED—AND IF my ears didn't deceive me, a tad jealous—that Isidor had treated me to lunch. "E.A.T., huh? He took me to the cafeteria in the basement," she said, nudging my shoulder as the train bumped along back to New Haven. "Isidor is something else, isn't he?"

"He's a character," I replied, thinking of the way he'd almost made me snort sparkling water out my nose at lunch. "Hey, do you mind if I tag along next time? I'd like to see him again."

"Just as long as you don't start critiquing my tour," she said, settling back in her seat. "Tell you what, as Professor Verhaast would say, I'd give half my kingdom to know what fascinates Isidor about *Young Woman with a Water Pitcher*. See if you can work on that, huh?"

IN THE END, IT WAS Danielle who tagged along, slipping out between tours to join Isidor and me for lunch. I cut classes and neglected my soccer practice to make the trip with her, and the three of us began to plan regular lunch dates, often in the coffee shop of the American Pavilion, which provided great fodder for our new favorite game, watching the museumgoers pass by. Danielle and I talked to Isidor about our plans to summer in Germany, and he, delighted, offered dozens of suggestions for the trip, including lists of cafés, museums, hotels, and emergency contacts.

It was easy to forget Verhaast in the company of Isidor, the old man was genuine charming and full of life.

By April, we were still no closer to learning the source of Isidor's fascination with the Vermeer, but it hardly mattered. The old man was a fount of stories, from anecdotes about pratfalls supposedly made by friends of friends of friends to remembrances of his late wife. He was in a fine mood one Thursday afternoon, discussing an exhibition of the Dutch Masters he'd once seen in Boston, when Danielle made her first misstep.

"My advisor—well, he's not officially my advisor, but you get it—Whitmore Verhaast? He talks about the Dutch Masters all the time in class," she said, sipping her Coke. "*Brilliant* lecturer, and he knows, like, *everyone* in the field. I mean," she said with a little laugh, "just last week, he had to skip class because he was in Amsterdam, trying to authenticate a Rembrandt. Anyway, he told us something interesting about Hals..."

I tried to tune her out—hearing Danielle gush about Verhaast made my blood boil—but when I cut my eyes to Isidor, I had to restrain myself from kicking her under the table. His face had tightened and cheeks slightly reddened, subtle changes but obvious to me. As Danielle continued to quote Verhaast, Isidor rose and excused himself to the bathroom, explaining, "When you're my age, ladies, you'll understand the urgency."

Danielle dropped the subject upon Isidor's return, and we parted as friends, but I could still see the tension in his shoulders. When we were settled on the train, I told Danielle, "You really shouldn't talk about Verhaast in front of Isidor. It upsets him."

"I don't see why," she protested. "Verhaast could tell him a thing or two about Vermeer."

Before we could argue, I steered the conversation toward a guy I'd met, Josh, who had apparently been grilling one of my freshman suitemates about me. "Sure, I know him," Danielle replied, brightening instantly. "He's the one who danced naked on the roof of Welch Hall last year, right?"

We spent the rest of the ride home talking about boys, and Danielle took upon herself to give me pointers. Nothing more was said about Isidor or Verhaast, but that night, I lay in bed and stared at the ceiling, almost feeling the weight of the crate beneath me.

ANIELLE DIDN'T LEARN OF MY LITTLE OBSESSION UNTIL WE were unpacking in our new dorm room junior year.

"What's that?" she asked, coming over to take a look at my milk crate. I tried to cover it up, but that only made the situation worse—she laughed, then snatched a stack of papers out of the back and danced across the common room while she scanned them. By the time she slowed and I was able to grab them back, her brows had knit. "These are all Professor Verhaast's articles," she said, sounding perplexed. "You're...doing a little light reading?"

"It's nothing," I muttered, and closed my bedroom door.

Several hours later, when I'd failed to show at dinner, Danielle pounded on my door until I poked my head out and found her with her arms folded. "I'm not going anywhere until you tell me what's wrong," she began. "If you're thinking about switching to art history—"

"I'm not."

"Okay, whatever. Look, Sabrina, I made you a sandwich. Would you please just talk to me?"

I hesitated, then pulled my door open

and crossed my arms to match hers. "If you really want to know," I mumbled, "then we're doing this right."

"What do you mean?"

"The peach schnapps," I said, pointing to our contraband bar. "Give it here."

ALTERNATING BETWEEN DRINKING AND CRYING—AND sometimes doing both simultaneously—I told her everything about my brief time with Verhaast.

"I was shopping his big lecture first semester," I forced myself to say, sitting cross-legged on our couch with the sandwich untouched on the coffee table and the schnapps bottle open in my hand. "Front row. I was hoping participation would help if the class was overbooked. He smiled at me."

Danielle waited silently while I composed myself.

"I signed up," I said in a shaky monotone. "He kept smiling at me. I went to his office hours. We got coffee. It turned into dinner. He bought us wine. We went back to his office so I could get my books…"

I could feel the leather couch under my t-shirt, the cold fingers on the waistband of my jeans, the fog in my head that told me fighting him off would be dangerous.

All of this, and more, I slowly told Danielle. By ten that night, I was drunk again and tired of crying, and she held me as she rocked us back and forth, whispering, "God, why didn't you *say* something?"

"You can't tell," I pleaded, grabbing her shoulders. "Promise me you won't tell!"

She gave her word, and then she put me to bed.

DANIELLE'S INTERNSHIP AT THE MET had ended, but I still arranged lunch that August with Isidor, who wanted to know all about our adventures along the Rhine. I must have seemed unusually subdued, because as we finished our coffee, Isidor took my hand and asked what was troubling me.

I took a steadying breath. "Isidor, what do you know about Whitmore Verhaast? It's important."

His dark eyes were still—not angry, not curious, just resigned. "He's an evil son of a bitch," he said quietly. "I don't use that term lightly." He paused, searching my face, then said, "I believe you know this already."

"I do."

Isidor shook his head and tightened his grip on me. "Then you should know as well that he's a *dangerous* son of a bitch, Sabrina."

He stared into my eyes—his meaning couldn't have been clearer if he'd had a flashing marquee.

"What do you mean, dangerous?" I asked, but Isidor just shook his head.

"Not here, not now," he murmured, and released me. "The time will come, dear. It will come."

IT CAME SOONER THAN I had expected—not from Isidor, but from his son.

A few days into September of my junior year, my phone had rung late one evening, and I'd looked down to see an unknown 212 number calling. New York, I knew, but my list of contacts in the City was limited to Isidor, and I feared the worst. "Hello?" I said, closing my bedroom door as I took the call.

The voice on the other end was brisk but warm. "My name is Walker Mendelssohn. Is this Sabrina Gutierrez?"

"Speaking," I said, sinking down onto my bed. "Oh God, did something happen to—"

"My dad is just fine," he soothed. "Sorry, I didn't mean

to scare you—Dad's perfectly healthy, all things considered, but he said you and I needed to talk. Would that be okay?"

I exhaled, realizing I'd been holding my breath. "Sure, uh... yeah, sure, Mr. Mendelssohn, that's fine. What's going on?"

"Please, call me Walker. And, uh..." He hesitated for a moment, then said quietly, "Would you be able to meet me at my office tomorrow afternoon? If your classes permit, of course," he added in a rush.

I smiled to myself, thinking of Isidor's stories of his grandchildren—two at Michigan, one at Princeton, and the free spirit of the bunch, a UCLA grad waiting tables in Pasadena while she worked on her screenplay. "No problem, tomorrow's my free day," I fibbed, figuring no one would miss me in my philosophy lecture class. "What time?"

He replied in a tone that forbade argument.

FROM MAPPING MY TRANSIT ROUTE from Grand Central, I'd gleaned that Walker Mendelssohn didn't exactly work at a starving startup, but even so, I was taken aback at the view from his corner office. The floor-to-ceiling window on one side of the room looked out over the Hudson River and the distant Statute of Liberty, while the glass wall opposite the window gave me a glimpse down into the firm's workings, a massive hall filled with banks of monitors and a beehive of traders. On the wall behind his desk hung a copy of *Young Woman with a Water Pitcher*—not a print, I immediately noticed, but a canvas. I had studied the painting at the Met several times, but this one looked different somehow, older and richer, even in the glare the afternoon sunlight filling Walker's office.

"Is that a Vermeer?" I blurted out.

"Yes," he said simply, but his eyes smiled.

"And the one at the Met?"

"A fake," he replied, adding, "Or if you will, an Isidor Mendelssohn."

My eyes darted back and forth between his faintly smiling face and the painting behind him. After a moment, Walker extended his hand toward a plush sofa. "Sit down, Sabrina."

I could not. I was transfixed by the *Young Woman With a Water Pitcher.*

"Sit down, Sabrina," he offered again, and to soften his abruptness, he walked around his desk and sat in the deep armchair beside the sofa, waving for me to join him. I noticed that he had picked the armchair with his back to the trading hall, giving him solely a view of the Hudson River.

A middle-aged secretary wheeled in a cart loaded with soft drinks, pastries, and coffee. While she was busy setting the cart, I heard Walker say, "My father doesn't like this place."

"Why?"

"He calls my work '*Luft Gisheft,*'" he answered, and both he and the secretary laughed. Seeing my confusion, he explained, "Yiddish for 'dealing with the wind.'" The secretary began to leave, and he said, "Martha?"

"I thought so," she replied, then pressed a button by the door. A cream-colored curtain slid silently along the glass, blocking the trading hall from view. She closed the door behind her, and Walker and I were left with each other, the cityscape below, and the *Young Woman with a Water Pitcher.*

"My father painted the one in the Met for Herman Goering," he said without preliminaries.

I felt that with this man, who sat on top of the world and traded in millions all day, being direct and honest was the proper route. He had the same build as his father without the warmth and the calmness that came with years. Walker was a bundle of controlled energy.

"What's the connection to Verhaast?" I asked.

Walker fixed himself a cup of coffee before replying. "My father warned me that this was what you're after," he said, but when he continued, he caught me off guard. "He has his own reasons why he wants me to tell you, and I will. But what's yours?"

"What?"

"Your connection to Verhaast?"

"He's a professor at Yale…"

"I know that," he interrupted, cutting me short.

His stare was at once penetrating and a warning—don't beat around the bush.

I willed myself not to get emotional. "I was in one of his classes freshman year, but I dropped it after he got me drunk and raped me."

Evidently, I'd caught him by surprise, "Rape?" he gaped.

"He paid for the abortion," I said matter-of-factly, but it didn't sound matter-of-fact to me.

"And Vermeer?" he interjected.

"Vermeer has nothing to do with me," I replied. "My business is with Verhaast."

We sat in awkward silence, each of us contemplating our drink. After a minute, I cleared my throat. "That's my connection, then. What's your dad's?"

He walked to the door, pressed the curtain open, and buzzed his secretary. "Martha, call Iris, please—tell her that Sabrina will be joining us for dinner." To me, he said, "I have some work to do. Where are you staying?"

He jotted down an address.

"I'd planned to go back to New Haven, actually—"

"Ordinarily, I'd suggest the Met until dinner, but something tells me you've seen enough art for the moment," said Walker, crumpling the note with the address and tossing it into a bin. "Tell you what, there's a Starbucks on the corner. Get your homework done, and I'll come get you when I leave. How's that sound?"

THE MENDELSSOHNS LIVED IN AN Upper East Side penthouse worth easily more than a hundred times my Yale degree, and I tried not to dwell on the fact that my mother's apartment could have fit into their family room. Still, Walker and his wife, Iris, were perfectly welcoming, and Iris poured a small glass of chardonnay for me as her husband finished making the salad and I took in the million-dollar nighttime view. When dinner was served, we gathered around the surprisingly cozy kitchen table in lieu of using the formal dining room, and as the bread and vegetables made the rounds, Walker told me his father's story.

ISIDOR MENDELSSOHN WAS A NEWLYWED artist when the Nazis invaded, conquered, and occupied the Netherlands. At the time, he was apprenticed in the restoration department of the Rijksmuseum with dreams of becoming a painter. He watched in horror as the Germans removed masterpieces off the walls of the museum, crated them, and shipped the load to Germany. They were methodical and discriminating. Every morning for weeks, a group of expert art historians and their handlers and officers would discuss the collection, frame by frame, and the ones deemed worthy were added to the list. Isidor was among the museum employees who were forced to assist, and when the Commandant learned that he was a German but only married to a Hollander, he was put in charge over his fellow workers. During one coffee break, he overheard the Commandant, who was a professor of art history at Heidelberg University, discuss Herman Goering's fixation with the women in Vermeer's paintings, especially with *The Milkmaid* and *Young Woman with a Water Pitcher*— but the conversation then slid glibly to lewd comments at the expense of the *Reichsmarschall* and his taste in women.

Mindful of the prize in the restoration department— *Young Woman with a Water Pitcher*, on loan from the Met, and knowing that it was just a matter of time before the Commandant would learn of its existence—Isidor slipped into the Rijksmuseum every night for weeks as the collection was pillaged, and made as faithful a copy as he could, even adding hints of grime to his artificially-aged canvas to give the appearance of a restoration in progress. When the job was finished, he carefully excised the true Vermeer from its frame, set the copy in its place, and sneaked the original out of the building in his satchel, which he buried in the cellar of his and Elsa's one-bedroom apartment. The next morning, Isidor presented the Commandant with the false Vermeer, claiming he had found it while cleaning the basement. Goering showered the Commandant with praise for a job well done, and in turn, the Commandant elevated Isidor as his personal assistant.

A jealous museum worker intimated to the Commandant that he was putting his own life in danger by protecting a Jew. Isidor and his wife were arrested the next day. His wife was exterminated as soon as the guards discovered that she was pregnant. Isidor was sent to a labor camp and then shipped to Auschwitz.

After the liberation, Isidor trekked his way back to

Amsterdam, retrieved his hidden satchel and left Holland, never to return. He reached America carrying the original *Young Woman with a Water Pitcher* in his suitcase, waiting for the moment to reveal the switch while rebuilding his life.

The people of the Netherlands purged themselves of the collaborators even before the smoke over Europe subsided. Many of the museum workers received long terms in prison and were stamped for the rest of their lives with a veritable mark of Cain and ended up pariahs. The colleague who had pointed Isidor to the Commandant, either out of shame or regret, spared Isidor when asked about his colleagues, and the courts exonerated Isidor.

"But my father has been haunted ever since," said Walker. "After my mother passed away, he began visiting his *Young Woman with a Water Pitcher*."

"When did she die?" I asked automatically and felt foolish a second later.

"Four years ago."

"Well, it's been four years since your mother passed away, honey," Iris corrected. "Isidor started to visit the painting two years and seven months ago."

"My mother is a bona fide third-generation American from Philadelphia," said Walker, sipping wine.

"Only on her mother's side," corrected Iris.

The detail didn't interest Walker. "Do you know, Sabrina, he took my sister and me to the Met hundreds of times, and never mentioned *Young Woman with a Water Pitcher*. My parents struggled to make ends meet most of their lives, and he had millions wrapped in a blanket at the bottom of the bedroom closet," he added as an afterthought; it was the first time I had detected a tag of emotion in his voice.

Iris walked to the other side of their kitchen island. "Coffee? Sabrina?"

"If you're having some," I answered. It was obvious that she wanted to break the rhythm of his thoughts; apparently, they had been at this point many times before. But I couldn't help mumbling, "If he was exonerated...the courts let him go..."

"There's no statute of limitation for Nazi collaboration," Iris explained.

And so Isidor held his tongue, leaving the Vermeer in its hiding place in his small apartment. He might have left it there indefinitely had his copy not returned to the Met in 1962.

Walker shook his head at the absurdity of it all. "It was the damnedest thing. I was four, so I didn't know why Dad was acting so strangely, but I remember him being upset about a story in the paper. He ranted in Yiddish, so I had no idea what was going on, but he kept re-reading these articles about the returned painting, and he must have made a dozen trips to the museum. I saw it when it first went back on display," he added with a sad smile. "Personally, I didn't see the fuss at the time. I was going through a dinosaur phase, and Vermeer didn't paint any dinosaurs."

The painting, he continued, went on several tours without incident. By 1972, however, finances were tight in the Mendelssohn house. With his daughter about to start at Barnard College and his son long overdue for braces, Isidor needed money, and he could think of only one solution: reveal the real Vermeer and hope for a reward, or at least honoraria for speaking engagements. His wife, who knew about the masterpiece in the closet, suggested that Isidor contact the young man who had authenticated the false Vermeer for the Met a few years prior. After all, she reasoned, he was a scholar looking for the truth.

So Isidor dialed directory assistance and located Whitmore Verhaast, the *wunderkind* from Yale who had been making such a stir among art historians of late. Though barely twenty-five, Verhaast had already completed his PhD, focusing on Dutch painting, and had made several very public authentications for museums and auction houses. With his boyish good looks and flare for PR, Verhaast was a natural in front of the camera and a genius in print, and had secured for himself a permanent position at the Met.

On an unseasonably warm April morning, Isidor entered Verhaast's office at the Met.

"Dad went through the whole story with him—the Rijksmuseum, the Nazis, the bag in the basement, the concentration camps—and then Verhaast snapped," said Walker.

I watched Iris reach over and gently squeeze Walker's left hand. His expression was distant, but the tension in his face spoke more of anger than fear.

"What transpired in that office, my father never told me or my sister, not a word. But years later, he disclosed that Verhaast warned him that if so much as a rumor of the truth came out, he'd expose my father as a Nazi collaborator."

"That man's a monster," Iris chimed in.

"Dad kept his silence all these years. Becky got a scholarship, I got braces later on my own dime, and after Mom died, Dad told us everything and gave me the Vermeer."

Walker hired a high-end research company to find out who, exactly, Whitmore Verhaast was. He told me briefly about the findings, warning me not to push Verhaast into a corner. Not, at least, as long as his father was alive.

Verhaast was a member of a secret corporation—"an art

cabal, a sort of art camarilla, if you will," Walker explained—that protected the investments of insurance companies, museums, and private collectors. "This secret corporation is a front to a society of old-timer Nazis who believe that the glory of Western Civilization is essentially German," said Walker. The cabal quickly silenced the source of any whiff of fraud.

"I suspect," said Walker, "that Verhaast knew that *Young Woman with a Water Pitcher* was a fake, but he didn't want to endanger himself." Walker sat down and smiled tightly. "Verhaast is a bit player in the whole thing, but he's smart enough to know he's expendable. If he'd let Dad bring the real painting out of hiding, then he'd have been discredited himself and, most likely, he knew the consequence. So, the best he could do to save himself was to hang this Sword of Damocles over my father's head as a Nazi collaborator."

He cleared his throat. "With Mom gone, Dad's had some time to think of late, and he's pretty much taken up residence with his painting. I know the whole damn thing sticks in his craw, but there's not much I can do about it. But I believe that secretly he basks in the praise and awe people lavish on his painting. If he makes a deathbed confession, so be it, but until then, if he wants to hang around the Met, I'm not going to stop him." He paused, then picked up his cup and sipped his cold coffee. "Sabrina, Dad wanted you to hear this because he's worried about you and Danielle. I'd say that anything more than superficial contact with Verhaast is inherently risky, and you...know more than is wise. Dad thought Verhaast was advising Danielle, and I'll be honest, that scares the shit out of me." He frowned into his cup for a brief moment, then stared at me with new intensity.

"Sabrina," I heard Walker say, and felt his change of

tone. "We had this conversation for one reason." He looked me straight in the eye. "As long as my father is alive, you don't touch Verhaast."

I matched his stare. "Vermeer has nothing to do with Verhaast and me—"

"I need your promise."

It was I who broke the eye contact to stare at my fingers. I would never dream of hurting Isidor; I also felt that Walker wasn't a person to be trifled with. When I returned my eyes to his, I realized he hadn't shifted his stare off of me, not even to blink. "You have my word," I said.

"Smart girl," said Iris.

"Not a word of this to anyone—not your parents, not your therapist, not your priest, not Danielle. Got it? Not a word as long as Dad is alive."

I nodded. "Of course."

"Thank you."

ALL THROUGH JUNIOR YEAR, I kept my silence. Danielle and I continued to meet Isidor for occasional lunches and coffee dates, usually at the Met, but I gave no sign that my meeting with Walker had ever occurred, and Isidor never mentioned it. My hatred for Verhaast never waned, but I knew that my grand—albeit hazy—plan to bring him low couldn't be tied in any way to the Mendelssohns. Walker didn't have to tell me that a group willing to murder to keep a secret wouldn't stop with Isidor. Isidor's children were in danger for knowing the truth—and now, I realized, so was I. And then Danielle disappeared.

ONLY A SPLIT-SECOND HAD PASSED BETWEEN STUMBLING UPON Hanna Deursen's gravestone and spotting another gravestone with 1675, the year of her death.

"Maybe Vermeer died in a plague," I said with as much levity as I could muster, pointing at the gravestone.

As I stood there in front of Hanna Deursen's grave while my new German companions talked about a lost painting and a female target, I tried desperately to put the pieces together.

Fredrick Krinsky: long-time curator at the museum attached to the Convent of the Blessed Virgin, disappeared without a trace from Het Klooster Stad, presumed dead.

Didrika Aken: Irish art critic writing on Fabritius and Vermeer, spent time in Het Klooster Stad, disappeared while returning from Amsterdam and an interview with Verhaast, presumed dead.

Danielle Carruthers: Yale senior, advisee of Verhaast, deeply interested in Fabritius's mistress, Hanna Deursen, disappeared during trip to New York, not dead if I could help it.

Hanna Deursen: virtually unknown mistress of a short-lived seventeenth-century Dutch painter, possibly a painter in her own right, most definitely dead.

Everything seemed to touch in some way on Het Klooster Stad and the convent. But *why?*

My mind raced as I stood there, shivering in the morning wind. The convent's biggest moneymaker had always been the Madonna and Child altarpiece, which might or might not depict the face of the possibly apocryphal miller's daughter. Maybe Krinsky or Aken had learned something new about its provenance, but I couldn't see that warranting the attention of an international thug squad.

I glanced down at the tombstone and frowned. What was Fabritius's mistress doing in Het Klooster Stad, anyway? Moreover, why was she buried in the convent's cemetery if she wasn't a nun? And she wasn't, I realized, peering at the inscription. The stones to either side of her clearly identified nuns—it didn't take a linguistic genius to translate *zuster*. Alone among the *Zuster* Marias and *Zuster* Marthes, why was Hanna buried here, under her birth name?

There had to be a connection to Verhaast—there *had* to be—but I'd be damned if I saw it yet. Why had he shown the slide of the mangled woman during his lecture, and why, out of the blue, had he asked me about Hanna Deursen afterwards? What did Hanna have to do with this place?

And most importantly, how was I going to get away from the Germans without arousing their suspicion?

With everything else I had heard I was ready to believe that the men who called themselves Hans and Fritz were working for the so-called art cabal. I needed to shake them, but more than ever, I knew I needed to break into Danielle's password-protected file—which, I realized, kicking myself for my carelessness, I'd left with the hunchbacked nun in the coffee shop.

Beside me, Hans pointed to the grave behind Hanna's. "Another 1675," he remarked. "Perhaps a bad winter."

"Maybe," I said, trying to keep my tone light. "Actually, I'm looking for a grave from the mid-fifteen-hundreds. Her given name was Helen. I forget the name she chose when she took her vows, but I'd know it if I saw it. You guys want to help me?"

My wild goose chase piqued their curiosity, and before long, I was telling the two all about myself—a senior from the University of Illinois at Chicago, researching the Dutch West India Company for a thesis in European history. "There's this story about a miller's daughter connected with the WIC," I said casually. "She was a Sister here, and I think she died in 1574. Chilly morning, isn't it?"

I walked on ahead, looking closely at each stone I passed. After a fruitless twenty minutes, Fritz muttered in German that he was wasting his time and made his excuses to me in English. Still, Hans lingered near my side, and when I couldn't feel my fingertips any longer, he suggested that we return to the village coffee shop and warm up. The look in his eye told me what other suggestions he had in mind, most of which involved his hotel bed, but I played dumb and let him escort me back to the tram.

I DIDN'T PICK UIC HAPHAZARDLY. I knew the campus pretty well. My mother had worked in the student cafeteria for years. When school was out and she had no money for babysitters, she would take me with her to work. Later, in high school, I discovered the university's library and was happy to exchange the corner table in the cafeteria for a stately, heavy reading desk. But no test followed. Hans couldn't care less where I went to school. He invited me to join him for dinner after I had given up locating Helen's gravestone. "It would be just a footnote in my paper anyhow," I told him, and accepted his invitation.

I knew that I was dancing a dangerous dance with Verhaast. The cabal was watching the convent, and I should have left quickly. Still, I wanted to learn about their operation. Maybe therein lay the clue to what had happened to Danielle. But Hans was either too good an agent or too dumb to know anything beyond his assignment, and I learned very little. I was careful not to ask a direct question, since as far as he knew, I didn't understand German. But I was patient, though my patience was heavily taxed. Mid-course at dinner, I made a mistake when I told him that I played intramural soccer. "Futball!" he exclaimed, and his eyes brightened.

When I left the dinner table, I knew more than I cared to know about the Futball-Bundesliga and how it was superior to the English Premier League, but not before Hans had invited me to his room. I clapped my hands over his and stared directly at his expectant eyes. "Hans, you're a good guy, I like you a lot," I said, "but I have to tell you, and I'm sorry I haven't told you before—I'm a lesbian."

He took his hands off the table quickly, as if he might be infected by a disease, yet he was careful not to offend me, and he even tried to salvage his night. "Some lesbians I know, especially athletes, are bi," he said hesitantly.

"Not me," I stated. "Sorry."

THE NEXT MORNING, IT WAS inevitable that we would share an awkward breakfast. I hadn't given up on finding out about his organization, and in particular his assignment at the Convent of the Blessed Virgin.

"About last night, Hans," I started.

"That's okay, Esther," he said, waving his hand. "I understand."

"Please, let me explain," I replied, then leaned over the table to whisper a great secret, though we were the only ones sitting on the veranda. "I'd love to hook up with you. It'll be fun," I said, and then, lowering my voice and touching his arm, I added, "I'm not a lesbian."

His eyes widened. "So, what was...the story of—"

"To cut off any argument. I, uh..." I tried to seem embarrassed. "I'm on my period."

His laughter caught me by surprise, a high yet guttural guffaw. He was relieved and hopeful again, and I almost pitied the guy. But the closest he came to revealing his business in the village was to confess that he couldn't talk about it. "You know, Esther, high-stakes insurance claims, banks, international institutions," he said, and then, so as not to appear rude, he added, "Frankly, we first thought that you were connected to our search, but, you know," he laughed awkwardly, "One day, I'll tell you."

"How can I get in touch with you?" I asked, carefully pouring syrup over my waffles.

He wrote a telephone number on a napkin. "Ask for Otto," he said.

"Otto?"

"It's a long story, Esther."

We parted friends, and I mangled the pronunciation of "*auf wiedersehen*." He laughed, and I let him kiss me on the cheek goodbye.

I flew back to the States that afternoon.

I RESUMED GOING TO CLASSES AND EVEN ATTEMPTED TO REJOIN the social life on campus. I participated in my residential college's intramural soccer game against our next-door rival—it was especially gratifying to me to score the winning goal, though I wasn't the one who set up the pass. A win is a win.

Only Josh knew how miserable and unhappy I was. "Sabrina, dear," he'd whisper, trying to console me, "Danielle is gone. It's sad, but she's gone."

Not for a moment did I end my efforts to break Danielle's password. There were a few computer geniuses around me whom I could have approached, but none who wouldn't connect the file to Danielle. I needed someone outside of the Yale community.

And then, a week after I returned, Verhaast summoned me through the dean. "He's been looking for you since you left," the dean explained, watching me with the tissue box at the ready.

"The poor guy probably wants to talk about Danielle," I said evenly.

I strolled by Verhaast's secretary twenty minutes late, sporting plaid flannel pants and a neon green ski cap and carrying an oversized cup of coffee from the bookstore across the street. "You rang?" I asked, stepping into his office; almost blaring out 'Hello from Hans and Fritz and maybe Otto.'

Verhaast looked up from his computer, startled. "It's called knocking, Sabrina."

"It's called giving a fuck, Whitmore." I plopped down in the armchair facing his desk and sipped my coffee.

He glowered back at me, then stood and closed the door. "You're late."

"Again with the fuck-giving." I turned and grinned up at him. "So, to what do I owe the pleasure of seeing your shining countenance once again?"

"To this," he said calmly, then turned his laptop around, revealing the painting of the mangled woman. "Have you seen this?"

"Oops, wrong slide," I mocked.

"Not this time," he barked from behind his desk. "Have you seen this painting?"

"Yes."

"Where?"

"At your last lecture, of course."

"Not the slide, the painting. The original."

I stared at the mangled woman in silence.

"Sabrina, this is important, please. Have you seen the original?"

I hadn't, but I wasn't about to tell him. I knew that this

was the painting the two agents of the cabal, Hans and Fritz, had been looking for. I kept my silence.

This heartbeat's pause turned out to be either an error or a home run. What followed was as humiliating and hurtful as his rape and the abortion. He threatened me. He'd see to it that I wouldn't graduate. "And who knows," he said aiming to hurt, "as far as I'm concerned, you killed Danielle out of envy. She was beautiful and smart and connected. You're dumb and ugly..." His voice trailed off, though he continued to seethe. "Has Danielle showed you the painting? Did she ever mention it?"

He fell silent, staring down at his desk, and then at me. His features relaxed, but not his eyes. When he spoke again, he spoke slowly and emphatically, pronouncing each word clearly and separately: "Have. You. Seen. This. Painting?"

I stood up. "Is that what you did to Danielle?"

The slap on my face wasn't as painful as the words that had accompanied it. I knew he had tried to control the swing halfway to my face, but the outburst was forceful. "You little wetback daughter of a whore! Yale should be ashamed to have you!"

THREE HOURS LATER, I FINAGLED my way through security and to the trading floor, and walked directly to Walker Mendelssohn's office. I had no recollection how I reached him, but I remembered well the blazing anger that propelled me on. Verhaast's slap hurt, but his words cut to the quick and reverberated in every cell of my body.

Daughter of a whore.

Christian missionaries brought my mother to this country to serve as an au pair to their three adopted Colombian children. They sponsored her legal papers to become a citizen and registered her for night classes to learn English. She was seventeen.

She gave birth to me in the emergency room of a Chicago hospital. My father was a Polish campus policeman who left the state the day my mother informed him that she was pregnant. The missionary family gave her twenty-four hours to pack. Being good Christians, they showed her the way to the nearest shelter.

Verhaast's words were intended to hurt, and he had succeeded beyond his wildest dreams.

"Sabrina," Walker exclaimed when he saw the look on my face, "what happened?"

"There's a file on this laptop secured by a password. I need it opened."

Apparently, there was something in my voice or in the way I had said it and in my appearance, which was, at best, wild—I couldn't control my humiliation and anger, and I hardly controlled my breathing. Walker typed a few words on his computer. A moment later, a chubby fellow in his late twenties entered the office. "What's up, Mr. M?"

"Brim, help this girl," Walker said, and handed him Danielle's laptop.

I followed Brim to his office off the trading floor. Four or five guys shared a long bench strewn with computers and keyboards and smartphones and gadgets I couldn't name, each man in a different state of slouching. They weren't traders, but rather the guys who kept the earth flat for the trading company. Brim slumped down on a swivel chair and turned on Danielle's laptop.

"The file's called 'Hanna Deursen,'" I told him.

A moment later I heard him mutter, "It's not protected."

"What?"

"Somebody removed the password," he said.

I stared at him and felt the world stop spinning. The only time that the laptop had been out of my reach was when the hunchbacked nun took my backpack to the kitchen.

"Did you let somebody fiddle with your computer?" I heard him ask.

"The hunchbacked nun!" I gasped, and covered my mouth with both hands so as not to scream, *Danielle*.

The five super-geeks stared at me, not knowing whether to laugh or call the paramedics for a straitjacket. Their confusion helped me catch my bearings. I dropped down into the nearest chair; I didn't trust my knees.

Somebody shoved a bottle of water in my hands, and Brim opened it for me when I failed to twist the top off. I sipped, and only then did I manage to whisper, "Are you sure?"

"Yeah," he said flatly, though his eyes were wary. "Don't worry—I made a copy of the file and saved it on your desktop and in your documents folder under the first word of the file." He glanced down at the screen, then said, "'Vermeer.' It's called 'Vermeer.'"

VERHAAST HAD EVERY REASON TO be hysteric in his anger and to fear for everything dear to him. His career, his reputation, and most likely every penny he owned would evaporate within a week of Danielle's paper's publication. He would be the laughing stock of academia and the art world, banned from museums and galleries, and forever disgraced and humiliated. In all probability, Yale would fire him, tenure notwithstanding.

That wasn't good enough for me.

Danielle's paper exposed Vermeer. She supported her research with the findings of Aken and Krinsky. It was solid research. Her paper was about Vermeer, and Vermeer had nothing to do with me.

When I read Danielle's Hanna Deursen file for the first time on the trip back to New Haven from Walker's office, and for the second time that night after a shower in bed, and then again in the morning, my plan began to gel. Verhaast's slap in the face only made it sweeter. The many variables that could derail my plan reeled in my head, and I devised contingencies. I left little to chance.

T EN DAYS AFTER I RETURNED FROM NEW YORK, HUGGING Danielle's computer with the file unlocked, my plan was complete.

The university registrar, with the help and support of the dean and my college's master—who, incidentally, was a distinguished professor of psychiatry at Yale Medical School, which helped my argument—stamped the required documents for my graduation. I would graduate magna cum laude—I was surprised to see that Verhaast gave me a B in his course; most likely a TA had put a W for 'withdraw' or F since I had missed the date to drop the course, Verhaast, however, in a moment of calculation to deflect attention from himself supplanted his TA letter with a B– and I resolved to find some way to rub it in Verhaast's face. The chubby Colombian girl was a straight A student.

I promised the master that I would return on time to march with my class on Commencement Day. "My mother will be under the tent, and that's a good incentive if I ever needed one," I explained.

The dean and the master, and my classmates, had recently been told that I had discovered cousins I hadn't known existed who had immigrated to Australia from Colombia the previous year. "You're a very courageous girl, Sabrina," said the master. Not articulated, but a constant presence during the deliberations, was the idea that connecting with lost family would compensate me for the pain of Danielle's disappearance. "It's a noble cause," said the master, and gave me a hug.

How could I tell them that I was burning to go back to the Convent of the Blessed Virgin to meet—and maybe hug—the hunchbacked nun? I couldn't; Verhaast was hovering around.

Josh had been on a mission of his own since I returned. While I was away, he had received an offer from the Boston Consulting Company for a position as an entry-level associate beginning in September. "Move with me to Boston, Sabrina," became his constant refrain. He implored me to apply to MIT or Harvard to get my PhD in math. He knew my dream and my GRE score, after all. "Come on, you've been talking about it for a year," he coaxed. "You're a shoe-in." When that didn't elicit the proper response, he tried, "After New Haven, Boston will be as good as New York," and finally, "Sabrina, we'll be together. Rent-free."

"Josh," I said, cutting him short one afternoon, "hold your horses."

He stopped abruptly, staring at me. I saw panic in his eyes, and I couldn't help but laugh. We were in the dining hall having lunch, and as soon as the senior table had cleared, he had leaned over to resume his argument, but he hadn't expected my quick interruption. "You're not breaking up with me, are you?" he almost cried.

"Josh."

"Yes?"

"I need your help."

"Anything. You know me."

It was heartening to watch his excitement. I trusted him. I started with Danielle's disappearance.

He listened closely without interrupting, and when I finished, he began to talk.

And that was the moment when I fell in love with him.

Josh had a special talent in hitting every step. He was the kind of guy who read instructions and followed them to the letter. When a chess game was over, Josh could point out the exact move that had sealed the outcome, but for the life of him, he couldn't have predicted or initiate it.

"Let me see if I understand you correctly," he began, and continued to summarize my plan in his clear and methodical way. It wasn't only money I needed—I was flat broke—but also a base, a solid center to back me up and rescue me if things didn't go as I planned. He was thoughtful and wholeheartedly forthcoming, lacing his summation with, "You're crazy," and "Why don't let the authority take care."

"Josh!" I cut him short.

He stopped.

I didn't tell him about the rape and the abortion.

One component of my plan was Danielle's computer. Walking with Josh to the dining hall, discussing my plan, I raised the question of the computer. To his credit Josh saw the weak link, and without a comment he held my hand, led me to the Apple Store on campus, and bought the latest model. He'd use the new laptop, and I'd take his. His laptop was a beaten, three-year-old workhorse and would pass a forensic test as a typical student's computer. Later, in my room, I transferred the decal of Helen I had bought at the Convent of the Blessed Virgin's museum from Danielle's computer to Josh's. During the following days, while putting my Yale affairs in order and enduring long discussions with the dean and the master about how best to meet my newly found relatives, I made the computer fully mine.

I created a "Vermeer Research" file and "The Miller's Daughter" file, and transferred most of Danielle's files—including, of course, the Hanna Deursen. I edited and rewrote sections in Danielle's paper. When finished, I formatted it to make it ready to submit for publication, then loaded it onto a flash stick and saved a duplicate on my hard drive.

Two days later, Josh gave me a credit card with my name backed by a giant hedge fund. "Just like that? So simple?" I asked incredulously.

"Dad's the second vice president of investment," he said, and dropped the subject.

The night before my leaving, I mentioned as casually as I could, "Professor Verhaast and I had a, uh…bad meeting. He might come looking for me before graduation."

"Should I tell him where you are?" he asked.

His question surprised me, but I didn't dwell on it. I let my silence stretch out, and just as he was about to break it, I whispered, "Yes, Josh, of course." And I returned his kisses.

THE DAY BEFORE MY FLIGHT to Antwerp, Belgium, I took the Metro-North train to Grand Central, and from there, I grabbed the subway to Brooklyn to visit Isidor.

"She probably went to Bazel," he said with a shrug.

"Basel, Switzerland?"

"No. Bazel, Belgium," he corrected me softly.

I shook my head. "What the hell would she be doing there?" I asked, more in despair than in surprise.

He stared at me with his dark, warm eyes, and I saw that the mischievous twinkle was missing. "I don't know where she is, Sabrina. If she went to Bazel…" He sighed. "If she doesn't return, you should tell the police about Bazel," he said, and stood there for a minute, shaking his head. His tone and the sadness in his voice frightened me.

"I don't know anything about Bazel!" I cried.

Probably he saw the fear in my eyes, as he finally said, "I know why you came here, Sabrina—you want a cup of tea." With that, his eyes twinkling once more, he walked to the kitchen.

The apartment was small and old but not musty. I looked around and mentally catalogued what I found: books and more books, photographs of Walker and Iris's wedding in silver frames next to identical silver frame of his daughter's wedding, a brass chandelier, photographs of the grandchildren, an old cupboard filled with crystal and porcelain, knickknacks, and embroidered pillows. The place had the feel of years and family and history—not a display of wealth, but certainly not an indication of its absence.

"Walker wants to buy me this fancy-schmancy condominium," called Isidor from the kitchen as if he had read my mind. "But I'm happy here. The subway is one block down the street."

He let me help him with the tray, a kettle, cups, and a dish of cookies. I took over the serving. While settling down, he in an armchair and I on a sofa, he mumbled, "Danielle, Danielle, she'll get into trouble if she's not careful."

My heart sank, but I said, "Isidor, what's all this about Bazel? Please..."

Isidor took his time preparing his tea, not looking at me, and then, quite softly, he began to speak.

BAZEL WAS A SMALL VILLAGE in Belgium, in the part of the country called Oost-Vlaanderen—East Flanders—during Vermeer's time. Its only mark of fame was a fifteenth-century castle, Wissekerke Castle, which drew a small but steady stream of discerning tourists. A woman named Paula Mertens and her husband, Wout Mertens, ran an antique store next to the castle; Isidor wasn't sure whether the Belgian Waffle Hut adjacent to the antique store belonged to the Mertens as well. "But the truth should be told, Sabrina," he added. "They make excellent waffles."

He paused, and when he looked at me next, his eyes became distant and cold, the way they had changed when he sent me to his son for the history of the *Young Woman with a Water Pitcher* he didn't or couldn't tell me himself.

Paula Mertens was the daughter of Fredrick William Krinsky, the now-vanished curator of the Convent of the Blessed Virgin's museum. Krinsky, Isidor murmured, was his colleague at the Rijksmuseum who informed the Commandant that he was Jewish.

I barely managed to control a gasp.

"When Fredrick came out of prison after ten years," Isidor continued, "he tried to get in touch with me. He knew that the *Young Woman with a Water Pitcher* Goering took from the Rijksmuseum wasn't Vermeer's. He had critiqued my work as it progressed and he gave me pointers. Krinsky was an expert on Vermeer. It still baffles my mind,

Sabrina, why Krinsky told the Commandant I was Jewish but not a word about the painting."

Isidor had no doubt of his fate had Krinsky disclosed the truth to Goering. "On the spot," he said, pausing to take a sip of tea. I could see his hand faintly shaking. "In the Rijksmuseum parking lot, I saw them doing it to another worker...a woman. They thought she was a member of the resistance..."

"He also didn't disclose it to the Met," I said, trying to draw Isidor back to the story.

He paused, staring vacantly at the wall above my head. I heard the cup clinking against the saucer in his hand, and I took them from him and put them on the coffee table before he could burn himself. "I'm sorry," I mumbled.

He recovered quite quickly, smiled, picked up the cup, and resumed his story. "This is a mystery, Sabrina. I don't know why he didn't go to the Met. He tried to get in touch with me several times, you know...but no. No. I couldn't... he killed Elsa..."

"Does Verhaast know about him?"

"Evidently," he said. "Nobody has heard from Fredrick Krinsky for how long?"

"Six years."

"Perhaps this was when Fredrick got in touch with Verhaast," he stated.

"I may stop in Bazel on my way to the village," I said.

"Just be careful, Sabrina. Just be careful," he almost whispered, then fell silent.

I RENTED A CAR AT THE ANTWERP AIRPORT AND DROVE SOUTH for less than an hour to Bazel, where I went through the motions of a perfect tourist. I took pictures of Wissekerke Castle, the lake, and the famous bridge, which was small and unremarkable but for its distinction of being the oldest suspension bridge in Europe. I had lunch at the Belgian Waffle Hut, a cheerful and sunny place overlooking the castle across the lake, and then I entered the antique store next door, a cluttered and gloomy place.

I'd done my share of flea market rummaging outside Chicago, so the cluttered interior didn't bother me, nor did the fine coating of dust on much of the merchandise. I sidestepped a rusting children's wagon, skirted a farm table loaded with oil lanterns and bits of carnival glass, and made my slow way toward the counter, an old blacksmith's bench adorned with leather bellows. As I got closer, I noticed a painting hanging behind the counter—and then I stopped in my tracks and stared.

It was the mangled woman.

The portrait Verhaast had shown at his lecture and shoved in my face was just a headshot, a small portion of the whole painting. The canvas was relatively small—no bigger than *Young Woman with a Water Pitcher* or *The Milkmaid*. I wondered why Verhaast had cropped so much out of his slide, and then, seeing the cobwebs around the frame, wondered if he knew what the piece looked like in its entirety. Probably that was all that Krinsky had shown him.

In the painting, the mangled woman stood in the middle of what seemed to be her boudoir, looking directly at the viewer. Two posts of her canopied bed were visible to her right. On her left, under an open window, was a wooden virginal with a white jug sitting on top. Behind her and partly obscured by her shoulder stood a painter's easel with an unfinished canvas. A torn map of the world was pinned on the wall. She wore an elaborate blue dress, a pearl earring, and a pearl necklace—jewelry that Krinsky had edited out of Verhaast's copy. In Verhaast's version, her right hand was lightly touching her collarbone, but here, her fingertips tenderly grazed her necklace.

In her left hand, hanging below her waist, and out of the slide, she held a shattered mirror that reflected fragments of her face in the shards of glass.

As I peered at the painting, I realized the setting wasn't boudoir or bedroom, but rather a multipurpose space—there was a globe on the floor beside the bed, a bowl of fruit on a table across the room, a stained palette propped against the virginal's spindly legs. I started cataloguing the items I found—pearls, musical instruments, maps...

I had seen this assortment before, in Danielle's painstaking list of objects appearing in Vermeer's paintings. And I had seen them in the Fabritius hanging in Danielle's parents' library and in the poster above her desk. The Fabritius might be a Vermeer after all, but Verhaast wasn't sure. Then again, he hadn't seen the original painting of the deformed woman.

I realized that I might be looking at an unknown Vermeer. And wondered whether Danielle has seen this painting.

Slipping around the counter, I stood on tiptoe to look closer at the shattered mirror. The mirror was smack in the middle of the canvas, keeping the structure of the painting in perfect balance. Seeing Verhaast's slide gave the impression that the painter wanted to shock us. Here, I felt that the woman in the painting had just discovered that her face was monstrously disfigured. Yet, she was not feeling sorry for herself. She was at peace. None of her deformities were reflected in the fragments. In the mirror, her face was as perfect and at peace as the faces of all the women in Vermeer's paintings.

The painting wasn't signed, but then I saw a faint line of text written along the edge of the mirror in red ink: "*Om te Iohannes.*" I'd never studied Latin, but one of my favorite scenes in *Indiana Jones and The Last Crusade* was when Indy tried to figure out the booby traps and get to the name of God. As he jumped onto a J tile to start spelling Jehovah, his father muttered that in Latin, Jehovah begins with an I. That made the last word *Johannes*—that, at least, I recognized as a name. A quick translation on my phone provided the rest: *All for you, Johannes.*

I don't know how long I stood staring at that painting, but I almost shrieked when I heard a friendly baritone behind me: "Don't fall in love with her. She is not for sale."

Whipping around, I found a burly blond about my age

standing on the other side of the counter, his face split by a wide, friendly smile.

"When the price is right, everything is for sale," I said, returning his smile.

He grinned. "You're an American, yes?"

"Yes, and passing through. A million dollars."

"Not even for ten million. It belonged to my *grootvader*, and my *moeder* won't sell it—"

"Fifty million."

"Now you're talking." He smiled widely, and I saw that he was badly in need of a teeth cleaning. "I saw you eating in the restaurant, so I can't offer you lunch, but would you join me for coffee? Before you pass through?"

"On one condition," I said, already accepting his offer.

"My *moeder* will kill me if I sell you the painting."

I laughed. "Okay, on to the second-best condition: Tell me everything you know about that painting." I stopped short of adding *and your grandfather*.

He nodded. "Not much, but I promise I'll tell you everything."

I offered him my hand. "Esther," I said, introducing myself.

"Jouke Mertens. My *vader* and *moeder* own the place." His huge palm swallowed mine, but his squeeze was soft. "Espresso? Café Americano?" he asked, and led me back to a table for two under a red umbrella outside the restaurant next door.

The young man running the waffle grill called out to him in Dutch, which I assume as close as to, "Jouke, you finally got a good one. Good luck."

Jouke answered in kind: "I need it. She's tough."

I couldn't control my blushing; I prayed it was slight. Seeing my face redden, he asked, "Do you understand Dutch?"

"No, but I knew you were talking about me."

It was his turn to redden. "Sorry. My friend is sometimes rude."

ON MY DRIVE OUT OF Bazel to the Convent of the Blessed Virgin, I separated his stories about the knee that he broke in the army, ending his dream of becoming a midfielder in the local football club, from the bits of information he told me about the painting and his grandfather. Whenever I stirred the conversation back to the subject, ever so hesitantly and with a by-the-way manner so as not to appear eager or single-minded, he always prefaced his comment with, "My *moeder* told me." His mother told him that his grandfather had found the painting in the dungeon under the convent. "They call it the Convent of the Blessed Virgin," he teased, "but in truth, they're all virgins there because they're so ugly, no man will sleep with them. My friend's girlfriend should join because she's so ugly—but alas, she's not a virgin." His laughter at his own witticism was pathetic, but I was a good listener and joined in his mirth. His mother told him that the woman in the painting was beautiful compared to the nuns.

"It's like Vermeer's *Girl with a Pearl Earring*," I replied.

"Who?"

I stared at him, barely containing my laugh of incredulity.

"More espresso, Esther?" he offered.

I accepted a refill. "So where's your grandfather now?" I asked.

His mother told him that his grandfather probably fell into a cave or a well, or locked himself into a cell in the convent. "He was a little crazy," he said, laughing.

That was indeed all Jouke knew about the painting and his grandfather. I promised to come back when his mother and father were home. "My offer to buy the painting still stands," I said. He walked me to my car.

Pulling out of the parking lot, I heard his friend hoot that once again, he had failed to score.

I reached Het Klooster Stad late that afternoon.

I MADE A NOISY RETURN, a mere three weeks after the first, and so I was known to the nuns in the museum store, at the coffee shop of the Pilgrim Inn, and at the semi-luxurious hotel the nuns ran. Josh had not only agreed to bankroll me, but had also suggested that I stay somewhere nicer than a hostel, and emphatically seconded my choice of accommodations.

"I hope that your sister who helped me before is still here," I said to the nun in the reception counter of the inn.

"We're all here to help you," she answered in accented English.

"She has... she is..." I wished I were a better actress, but then I blurted out, "She's hunchbacked."

The nun paused a fraction of a second before answering, "Yes. She's still here."

Hans was sure that I had returned for one purpose: to sleep with him. I kept his hopes alive at dinner—he was an important link of my plan, my conduit to the head of the cabal—I explained to him that my return trip was due to my stupid research adviser, who said that in order to complete my paper, I needed to provide proof that Helen von Leinsdorf, the miller's daughter, was indeed buried in the convent cemetery.

Hans, of course, had only one thing on his mind—but he apologized that his investigation of an insurance fraud scheme prevented him from accompanying me to the cemetery. "We still looking for a missing painting and a woman who most likely stole it," he disclosed. His stint in the village was coming to its end, and a replacement, another investigator, might arrive soon.

"Fritz is returning?" I asked as nonchalantly as I could fake.

"I don't think so. Maybe Monica," he said, and then hinted that our opportunity to sleep together was growing short as well. "I can't stay here," he lamented.

I held his hand. "Once I find this fucking gravestone, I'll travel with you anywhere you need to go," I promised, and he was mightily satisfied.

I TOOK THE FIRST TRAM in the morning up to the Chapel and walked directly from the tram station to the cemetery. And there, waiting for me by Hanna Deursen's gravestone, stood the hunchbacked nun. She turned her back to me, crouched, and began to weed.

"Hi," I said.

"Don't scream," said Danielle, "help me with this."

I bent down. Our hands touched, and she squeezed mine. "Stay calm," she whispered.

"I'm about to wet myself," I said, trembling.

"Wouldn't be the first time," she whispered, and I heard that she, too, was sniffing. "What took you so long?" she added, the relief evidence in her voice, but then she whispered, "Take a piece of paper out of your bag and ask me for directions."

I did.

She pointed deeper into the cemetery, up the mountain and along the wall of the convent, then walked off in that direction. I followed. Her coarse, black habit caught in the weeds here and there, but she yanked it loose and kept on walking. At times, she forgot to limp. She was also seemingly muttering to the wind: "They're following you. They're professional killers. Don't let on that we know each other…"

I walked close enough behind her to keep my voice low. "You're a ruthless fucking bitch. I thought you were dead."

"I was a day or two ahead of them."

"Who *are* they?"

"The people who employ Verhaast."

We kept climbing along the wall, going faster and faster as if in a trance.

"How far do you want to go?" I asked.

"I have no idea." She laughed softly, choking back a sob, but didn't stop or turn.

We kept on walking.

"Let's find Helen's gravestone," I suggested.

"Who?"

"The miller's daughter."

Danielle shook her head. "She's buried in the chapel."

"Yeah?"

"Do you remember the year that she died?"

"You wrote that she was born in 1536 and died in 1574," I said.

She stopped, but only after glancing around for watching eyes. "Give me the piece of paper," she said. I handed it over, and she stared at the blank paper, then bent to read the date on the nearest gravestone. "Fuck, we're in the thirteen hundreds." She straightened up and pointed back and down the slope.

We cleaned and cleared the gravestone of Henrietta Olinda Ansel, Zuster Magdalena, who died in 1555. "Close enough," Danielle decided when we reached the mid-sixteenth century. We cleared and weeded, and we talked and talked. We laughed, we cried, and sometimes we argued with poor Henrietta or a stubborn weed, but never directly addressed each other.

We were scared.

I snapped pictures as the work progressed, and she, making a show of being the perfect, demure nun, stepped out of the frame each time. At times, I couldn't tell whether she was crying or smiling; the slit for her eyes was too narrow.

While cleaning mid-sixteenth-century gravestones, I told Danielle about the cabal. She knew about the professional killers she called "Verhaast's company." "*Cabal* is a better term," she conceded; she was mildly surprised at how deeply Verhaast was involved. She had connected some dots, though. Back in her sophomore year, Verhaast tried to dissuade her from researching Hanna Deursen. "I found a slide Krinsky had sent him years before. He kept the slide locked away," she told me in one of her less panicked moments. "It's Deursen's self-portrait. She was here. She lived here for thirty years. She painted here. Krinsky might have found her studio. My paper is worth nothing if I don't find the studio. I'd give half my kingdom, all my kingdoms to find it." We chuckled at the reference. "What's that saying about curiosity and cats?" she muttered, scratching at the hard ground. "When I figured out who Verhaast was talking about, I feared for my life."

"Why the fuck didn't you tell me you knew?" I protested.

"Why the fuck didn't *you* tell me *you* knew?" she repeated angrily.

I said nothing. How could I explain to her that my objective had never been to reveal the truth about Vermeer?

We continued to weed and dig dirt out of letters as if we really meant it. I finally broke the silence to mutter, "I don't think they see us."

"Don't fool yourself, they're professionals. You know what happened to Aken and Krinsky, I saw the clippings in your milk crate. Trust me," she said, and I felt that the tension between us had passed.

"How did you find out?" I asked.

"Krinsky, Didrika, Isidor."

"Isidor?" I was stunned.

Danielle shook her head. "You have no idea, Sabrina. We might end up here together for the rest of our lives."

She told me that Verhaast did report the story of Isidor and *Young Woman with a Water Pitcher* to the cabal. "But they concluded that it was an isolated problem between the Met and Verhaast and that it wouldn't affect the rest of the Vermeers. Isidor was Verhaast's problem."

I told her briefly about the threat Verhaast had used to keep Isidor silent, using Walker's image of the Sword of Damocles. "He's a monster," said Danielle.

"You're telling me," I replied.

We laughed tensely, and then she got into one of her spins of despair. "I told Mother Superior that I came here to research Hanna Deursen, I even cleaned her gravestone... Sabrina, Mother Superior agreed that I could hide here for three weeks, and now she's pressuring me to leave or commit," she said, choking back a sob.

"To mutilate yourself?" I asked in shock.

She didn't answer, and then whimpered, "I knew that

you were the only one who would trace me here. But Sabrina, I'm stuck...I'm scared..."

This was the moment when I decided to execute my plan as soon as I was back in the Inn.

THE SUN BEGAN TO SET. The valleys among the mountains were already dark; here and there I could see lights in the distance. By the time we departed, five gravestones had been cleaned, and our hands were cut and dirt was caked under our fingernails. Danielle entered the convent through a wooden door in the massive medieval gate, and I took the last tram down to the village.

I couldn't tell whether I was followed.

I entered the coffee shop and momentarily panicked when I didn't see Hans. When I had decided to initiate my next move as soon as possible, tonight if I was successful, Hans was almost central to it success. I hadn't planned it for tonight, and Josh wasn't expecting it, but Danielle was at the end of her rope. Her mood oscillated between cool and despairing. Her highs inspired me. Her lows frightened me.

She feared for her life. She had evaded the goons of the cabal, but she had no idea how to get out of hiding and drop her disguise, brilliant as it was. "I managed to run away," she whispered to a stubborn thorn bush, "but I'm stuck, Sabrina, I'm stuck. If I leave, they'll kill me. If I stay, I'll die." She whimpered and tossed the bush into our pile of uprooted weeds. At one point, when she was more lucid and calmer, she said, "If I can't find physical evidence to support my paper, Hanna Deursen is as good as a name on a gravestone like the rest of these poor women." She waved her hand, encompassing the entire cemetery. "And then Verhaast will kill us both."

I didn't tell her my plan, of course, but now I had to move fast.

My first call was to Josh, but I only reached his voicemail. "It's me," I said in a quiet rush. "The game's afoot tonight. I'll explain later. Love you." Only after I had cut the connection did I realize what I had said in farewell. It was the first time I had said those words. Maybe I had been in love with him for a long time—but this wasn't the time to reflect.

My next call was to Hans. I was prepared to sleep with him if need be, and, steeling myself, I dialed the number he had jotted on the napkin. A woman answered in German on the second ring. "May I speak with Otto?" I said in English.

There was a slight hesitation, and then she replied in impeccable English, "Who gave you this number?"

"Hans."

"Hans?"

"Maybe Otto?"

"Who are you?" she snapped

"I'm Esther, Hans's friend from the Convent of the Blessed Virgin. He told me to ask for Otto," I said.

The woman's voice was suspicious. "Are you one of the nuns?"

"Not yet," I laughed, though it was close to a possible outcome.

"You're lucky," she said, warming up to me. "Esther... your name is Esther, yes?"

"Has been since the day I was born," I said, and didn't forget to giggle.

She laughed. I knew they were checking the callback number and maybe triangulating my cell phone's location.

"Esther," she asked, "what message would you like to leave for Otto?"

I played dumb. "Actually, I wanted to speak with Hans."

Her voice changed, now as condescending as if she were talking to a kindergartener. "Okay, Esther, what message did you want to leave for Hans?"

I took the plunge. Giggling, I said, "Tell him that I know who Vermeer was."

"Vermeer?"

"Yes, I know all about him. And I know why Hans is in the village. I can help him."

"Did he tell you?"

"Tell me what?" I asked, continuing my ditzy act.

"Did Hans tell you why he was in the village?"

"I figured it out myself. *Duh.*"

She swallowed. After a long pause, she put me on hold for a moment, then returned and asked sharply, "Can Otto get in touch with you at this number?"

"Actually, I'm looking for Hans." My tone said, *How stupid you could be?*

There was another long pause, and then she said, "Okay, Esther, Hans will call you."

"Awesome. But tell him my battery is getting low. Tell him that I'll have dinner in the restaurant at the inn. He knows where that is. Oh, gosh, what's the time now…tell him I'll be there at eight-thirty…"

"He'll be there, Esther."

After a few more clarifications and some bantering, we hung up as friends.

They knew where I was.

I had half an hour to take a shower. I used every drop of the shampoo and conditioner the hotel provided, then smeared on a generous squeeze of body lotion, hoping that the heavy floral scent would convince Hans that I had bed on my mind. I still hadn't quite figured out what to tell him. Three stories were dancing in my head when my telephone began to vibrate. It was Josh.

"Sabrina, I didn't expect—" he shouted as soon as I said hello.

He, most likely, was glowing because of that one little word I'd let slip. But I cut him short. "Josh, trust me. I have to move tonight. It's eight-twenty here, and I've got to get to dinner. I'll explain later."

"Should I send the tickets?"

"As we planned. Only the timing has changed."

"You know me," he said.

"I trust you, Josh."

"Hey, Sabrina, Verhaast had dinner in the college last night—he was looking for you."

"Tell him where I am," I said.

"So soon?"

"We're running out of time."

There was a slight pause, then I heard him say, "I will, Sabrina," and he started to ask questions.

"Josh, Josh, not now. I have to go. Thank you. Love you," I said, and hung up.

I was sure he was staring at his telephone, trying to determine whether he had heard me correctly. Sitting naked on the bed, I texted, *Call me in fifty minutes. Love you*, and pressed send.

I didn't dry my hair or wear a bra. I put on a t-shirt, and for once I was grateful and not self-conscious of my full breasts. I took the elevator to the restaurant to meet Hans.

WE WERE BACK IN MY room in twenty minutes. My wet hair and the fragrance of the shower telegraphed to Hans my unequivocal consent. The bulge in his pants swelled the moment he bent to kiss my cheek. We sat down in the restaurant and ordered wine, and I told him that I had to leave the next day. "That was why I called Otto," I said, fluttering my eyelashes in what I hoped was a coquettish fashion. "I wanted to see you tonight..."

"Shall we skip dinner?" he suggested more than asked.

"We can always eat later," I said, standing, and leaned on his shoulder for balance.

In the elevator, I let him kiss me on the mouth.

"Why do you have to leave tomorrow?" he asked, catching his breath.

I shrugged, belittling the importance of my reply. "Small trouble. Nothing I can't solve in ten minutes."

"If it's small, why the rush?"

On our way to my room, I told him the truth as I had prepared it, one of the stories that had danced in my head. His cooperation was essential to the success of my plan.

Before taking the elevator down to the restaurant to meet Hans, I put my laptop in my knapsack, tossed the knapsack onto the armchair by the bed, and threw a bra over it. The disguise was flimsy, but that was the point, after all.

I made a full production of unlocking my room and bolting the door behind us while prattling on. When things were secure and Hans's physical interest had become quite visible, I froze, covered my mouth, and whispered, "*Shit!*"

Hans paused, one arm out of his jacket. "What's wrong?"

"The file! I forgot all about it! Oh, shit, *shit*...I am so *screwed*, I'm going to lose my apartment—"

He grabbed my arm to stop my sudden pacing. "Esther, what's going on? What's the trouble?"

I took a deep breath, choked back a rather convincing sob, and willed tears to my eyes. "There's this nun, okay? She's doing some research for a professor, something on whatshername—you remember that grave we saw? Nanna Dores?"

Hans frowned at me. "Hanna Deursen?"

"Yeah, that's it. Well, the professor's in a rush, and the nun said she'd give me five hundred bucks—five hundred Euros, whatever—if I'd send him the file today. They don't have internet at the convent," I said with a shrug. "She was going to give me the money once I sent the e-mail." I forced my eyes to water. "So...so she gave me the file on a flash stick, and I transferred it to my computer, but I don't know where it *went*! I can't find it! I was going to keep looking for it, but then I got to talking to you..." I let my voice trail off and folded my arms, hugging myself as I sniffed.

Playing dumb was easy. Whenever I helped my mother with officials, filling in this form or that, dealing with her landlord or welfare agents—everyone expected me to be an idiot, and I had honed being stupid to almost perfection. Now, I employed my technique to its fullest.

"I need the money, Hans. My rent's due, and if I don't get it to my landlord by morning, he's going to kick me out, I *know* he will, he's a complete asshole. But I've looked everywhere, and I can't find the file!"

"Don't worry so much," he soothed, resuming his disrobing. "Your landlord won't mind if you're a day late, and this nun and her professor—they can wait a little longer, can't they?"

I shook my head. "She said he'll go ballistic if he doesn't

get it today. Some guy named Verhaast, he's a big-shot at Yale, thinks he shits gold or something."

The bulge in Hans's pants disappeared. "Who's this nun, again?"

"I don't know. They've all got those stupid veils."

"What's her name?"

"Sister something... I don't know."

My suitor had suddenly become the cabal's soldier. Good. But too early. I had to work on more credibility.

"Oh, screw it," I exclaimed, throwing my hands in the air. "You're right, it'll keep until morning. Come here, you." And without ceremony or preliminaries, I took off my t-shirt and trusted my breasts to do their job.

The bulge reappeared almost on cue, and I unbuckled Hans's belt. His hands couldn't resist my bare chest, yet he managed to mumble, "What's it about?"

"What's what about?"

"Verhaast's research."

I sighed impatiently. "The nun said something about that Vermeer painter guy not actually being Vermeer, but I don't know. Who gives a fuck?" I said, and pulled his pants down. His bulge sprang forth, and he quivered when I touched him. I bit his earlobe and whispered, "Take a shower," implying great things to come.

Josh, call me now, I prayed.

Hans didn't close the door to the bathroom, but the shower turned on. While I contemplating whether to put my shirt back on or take off my pants, my telephone vibrated. Josh. I cut the call off and frantically set the telephone back to sound. After three seconds of silence, it rang again. *Josh, I love you*, I reflected, and called to the bathroom, "It's mine!"

The water turned off.

"Hello?" I said to the telephone.

"Sabrina, it's me, what's up?"

I didn't answer. I listened, more to the bathroom than to Josh. Poor Josh was shouting as if the connection was bad. I listened, but there wasn't a peep from the bathroom.

"Sabrina, is everything alright? Sabrina, talk to me..."

Finally, I said, "Okay."

"You don't sound so good, hon. Are you there? What's going on?"

I kept silent, and silence was in the bathroom. Finally I said with resignation:

"Okay. I'll do it now."

I cut the connection and turned off the telephone. The hiss of the water resumed.

A short time later, Hans walked out of the bathroom with a towel around his waist. The towel barely covered what was on his mind—it seemed Vermeer and Deursen could wait. But I was crying. I was sitting on the bed, my breasts exposed, my pants pulled down, ready to make love—but I was crying.

"What happened?" he asked.

I blubbered, though I was careful not to exaggerate. "Fucking Verhaast, that's what! That stupid nun gave him my number, and he wants the file *now*. 'Time is of the essence,'" I mimicked in a falsetto. "Fuck that."

Hans sighed. "Don't cry. You need the money, we'll send the file now. Okay?"

"I told you," I said, putting a tremolo in my voice, "I don't know where it is! Oh, shit...maybe if I take my computer back to Chicago, someone at school can find it..."

"That's silly," he said impatiently. "I can help you right here."

"Would you? Great!" I said, flashing him what I hoped were baby seal's eyes, then took my laptop out. "Do you know computers?"

He made a face as if having a better thought. "My colleague does."

"Fritz?"

His interest shrank dramatically, and he realized that he was standing stark naked in front of me. "Let me call him," he said, walking back to the bathroom, where he had left his clothes and, presumably, his telephone.

A moment later, I heard him speak in German "She's fucked up, the stupid bitch," he began as he explained the coincidence of the file on my computer. He called Verhaast *"der kunstberater"*—"the art expert"—in an unmistakably derisive tone, then listened. "I don't have to steal it! She practically begged me to take it." He listened again. "You have to help her e-mail a file," he said, failing to disguise a sneer. "Dumb cow saved it to the wrong folder probably with the wrong extension and doesn't know how to run a damn search."

He was beyond pity.

Hans walked out of the bathroom with his pants on, holding the telephone. "My colleague is already in bed, but he doesn't mind if I bring him the computer. Do you mind?"

"Oh, would you? Go ahead."

On the telephone, he said in German, "Ten minutes," and added in English, trying lamely to joke, "Make yourself decent."

"That's okay," I said quickly, then shook my shoulders,

letting my breasts wiggle. "Go ahead, I'll wait in the restaurant. I'm famished."

When he left with the computer, I almost danced a jig, then realized that the idiot hadn't asked me what file to send, and to which address. Most likely, his colleague would realize the slip, or they might assume that the ditzy Esther wouldn't have a clue.

I changed into a decent shirt, combed my hair, and allowed myself to smile in the mirror.

BEFORE HEADING BACK DOWNSTAIRS, I turned on my telephone. Sweet Josh had filled my inbox with anxious messages. I texted him back, making the message clear and explicit: *I'm fine. Everything is better than I expected. Love you.*

I turned off the telephone and walked to the elevator. The bottle of wine Hans had ordered and the two half-filled glasses were still on the table. Only a few diners sat here and there; none, to my relief, were on the veranda. The serving nuns knew—or at least tried to imagine—what had transpired in the interval since our departure; they stared at me through the narrow slit in their habits with eyes full of admonition, or perhaps envy. I sipped my wine with relish and, I had to admit, to collect my bearing. Hans's colleague, the mysterious Otto, who I imagined was reading Whitmore Verhaast's definitive paper on Vermeer as I was sipping, might not be as single-minded or easily duped as Hans. Secretly, I hoped that Otto would have the authority to execute my next move. He might do so soon after reading Verhaast's introduction, which I had inserted into the paper. It was a thing of beauty, a scholar's blend of mea culpa and eureka, filled with key phrases like, *"I'm well aware of the shudder and, I dare say, revolution in the art world,"* "the consequences to my reputation and academic life," and, "the overwhelming scientific findings, verified and authenticated, compel me to submit this paper."

I also changed Danielle's title, which was a convoluted two-line scholarly jumble to "Vermeer's Self-Portrait." Of course, I made Whitmore George Verhaast the sole author.

I mentally accompanied Otto's eyes as he read while I silently sipped my wine and waiting for dinner.

FIFTEEN MINUTES LATER, I WAS startled by Hans's hand on my shoulder, as if claiming his property, "Esther, dear, this is Otto."

I jolted off my seat to meet Herr Otto Werner Kuhn. He was bald, stout, and middle-aged, with thick fingers and eyes heavy with gravitas that bored through me. I turned to shake his hand, but with a swift and innocent-looking motion, I knocked over my glass of wine. A large red stain splashed on the white table linen. During the ensuing commotion, I had time to size up Otto and turn back into the ditzy Esther. I sensed authority. Otto walked over to one of the nuns, who didn't clamor to clean up the mess, pointed at a table in the corner, and sat down. He put my laptop in front of him, and I joined him.

"Did you send it? Did you? Tell me that you sent it," I gushed.

Hans stopped apologizing to the nuns for his girlfriend's clumsiness and rushed to our table. "Yes, we sent it."

"Awesome!" I clapped my hands with joy and grabbed the laptop. "I'll e-mail Verhaast to tell the nun to give me the money."

My sudden reach across the table startled Otto and shocked Hans.

Otto put his heavy hand on the laptop I had already flipped open and pushed it closed, almost nipping my fingers. At the same time, he asked Hans in German, "Does she know why we're here?"

"What?" I said.

"Esther, the e-mail can wait," Hans said, and placed the laptop back in front of Otto.

I scowled. "I told you, I need that money—"

"The banks are already closed in America," reasoned Hans.

"No, they aren't, and I know my landlord, he'll evict me if my check bounces. I have to tell him—" I reached for my laptop with as much panic as I could fake.

"Esther," said Otto. The sound of his voice made the world stand still. "We'll give you whatever money you need."

"What? Why?"

"If you're a good girl and answer a few questions, we'll give you money."

"Hans, please," I said, using my brown eyes to full effect once more.

"Forget about the money, Esther," Hans said to me, and to his colleague in German, "Don't you see that this is the most important thing in her life? Let her send the damn e-mail."

Otto ignored Hans, who evidently had only one thing on his narrow mind.

"Esther," I heard Otto say, "Esther, can you introduce us to this nun friend of yours?"

"What nun?"

"The nun that gave you this paper."

"She didn't give me any paper."

"What did she give you?"

"A flash stick with a file on it."

"Yes. Good. Who is she?"

"How would *I* know? She died at the same year as Vermeer!"

"Not Hanna Deursen, the nun!"

It was Hans's turn to put his hand on Otto's shoulder to calm him down.

"Aren't you wondering," said Otto in German, controlling his anger, "whether the woman we've been looking for might be the nun that found this dimwit? And what about the marvelous coincidence that this fat *schwartze* found you?"

"Pure coincidence and our luck," answered Hans in German. I was surprised at his equally commanding tone.

"Okay, coincidence, but that the"—he paused, searching for a word—"that *der kunstberater* first recommended to our client that we take care of his student, then alerted his student that she was in danger, then suggested that the student might be here in this damn village..." Otto paused to swallow, then stared at me and at Hans. "And on top of everything, this idiot works for *der kunstberater*—"

"She doesn't work for him—"

"What's the difference? She's mailing him things, isn't she?"

I pretended that I had failed to catch the words *idiot* or *schwartze*. "What's wrong?" I asked.

Otto continued in German, ignoring me. "The client will deal with *der kunstberater* as they see fit—we'll get the job anyhow, but right now, we were hired to find the girl."

"What *is* it?" I interjected, and added quietly, "It's not polite to speak German when you know I can't understand you."

They ignored me.

Hans replied in German, "It's a coincidence."

"We need to make sure," Otto replied. To me, he asked in English, "What brought you here?"

"Well, I took a plane to Antwerp—"

"Esther," Otto said, cutting me short, then composed himself. "I mean, why did you come here, to this village?"

"Do you think I wanted to? My stupid professor wants a picture of Helen von Leinsdorf's gravestone!"

"Who's that?"

"Hans knows. I told him—"

Hans interrupted me in German; I was surprised that he summarized my research quite nicely. He concluded, "She has only two things in her empty head: taking a picture of the gravestone and the money the nun owes her."

"How do you know all that?"

"I already fucked her," said Hans.

Once again, I was surprised to see Otto laugh silently, like a proud master pleased with his pupil's achievement. Then he turned to me and spoke slowly. "Esther, dear, have you read the article?"

"Of course I read it, I wrote it! How stupid do you think I am?" I was so indignant that I surprised myself.

"Esther, dear, I'm sorry, I don't think you're stupid, I think you're very smart. I meant Professor Verhaast's article."

"Which one?"

"The one on Hanna Deursen. The one on your computer."

"Hell, no! You think I have nothing else to do? Verhaast is such an ass—I looked at, like, the first page, and I almost fell asleep. And I'm getting tired of this conversation," I said, reaching for my laptop.

Otto put his thick hand on the computer.

"Hans, please, tell him! I need the money!"

Otto spoke gravely, apparently having decided to change

his tactics. "Esther, an insurance company hired us to find a missing Vermeer painting."

"How is this my problem?"

"We think that a student of Verhaast's stole the painting. You can help us find her."

"Who?"

"The student."

"I don't know any of his students!"

Otto sighed deeply and rubbed his temples, apparently on his last nerve with me. "Esther, listen: the nun who gave you the file you wanted e-mailed, what's her name?"

"No clue," I replied. "I was praying in the chapel, and she knelt next to me and promised to give me the money if I'd mail a document to Verhaast, and then we went back to her room and loaded it onto my computer, and I left—"

"Slow down, Esther, slow down—"

"Now I want my money," I concluded, pleading, almost crying.

Hans tried to intervene, but Otto cut him off. "Have you seen this picture?"

My dinner arrived. Two silent nuns unloaded a tray with dishes I didn't order, and a third one, the maitre d', stood aside, supervising. I could swear she was Danielle without the hunchback. Otto and Hans followed the nuns like foxes in the wood to catch a hand gesture, body language, eyes contact—all in hopes of detecting familiarity— but the two nun-waitresses walked away as silently as they had appeared, and the maître d' I thought was Danielle asked me with French-accented English whether everything was to my satisfaction. I nodded, afraid to speak or look at her. I hadn't ordered any of the dishes on the table, none was on the menu, but each was my favorite. She asked in a ridiculous French accent English whether my friends wanted to order as well.

"They speak English," I said, staring at my plate.

Hans ordered salad. Otto politely declined.

"Be careful, madam, the lentil soup is very, very hot," she said, and walked away.

"Have you seen this picture, Esther?" Otto asked again as soon as the nun-maître d' had left.

For a moment, I thought he would show me a photo of Danielle, and I was ready to swear that I had never seen her, but he showed me a print of the grotesque woman's headshot instead.

"Uh, *ew*," I said.

Otto fought to maintain his composure. "Yes, we know. Have you seen it?"

"What's so important about that painting? It's like a Halloween mask."

I tasted the soup, remembered it should be hot, then pantomimed a burned tongue. "Oh, *wow*, that's hot, excuse me. God, she wasn't kidding! Sorry, what were you asking?"

"Have you seen this picture?"

The maître d' appeared with Hans's salad. "Will this be all, madam? We're about to close the kitchen for the night," she said, the French accent thick and bordering on the absurd.

"I'm all right," I murmured to the soup.

"I hope so," she said. "Gentlemen?"

They nodded and waved politely that they, too, were all right.

When she left again, Hans surprised me by speaking. He spoke slowly, touching all angles to prevent any misunderstanding by the dumb Latina.

"Esther, dear, the nun who gave you the computer flash stick, the nun who asked you to send the file to Professor Verhaast, the nun who promised you five hundred bucks to send the file, the nun—"

"That's all the same nun," I said with glee, as if catching the trick.

"Yes, Esther, it's the same nun. Did she show you this picture?" he continued emphatically.

I took a closer look at the picture and made a face. "Is that her picture? Poor thing. No wonder she wears that veil."

He ignored my remarks. "This painting has been missing for quite some time, Esther."

I looked up at Hans, feigning impatience. "So? What does that have to do with me?" After a brief pause, I asked, "You think that has something to do with the nun, don't you? Guys, whoa, you've got it all wrong. She's working on Vermeer. Look, I'm no expert, but even *I* know that ain't a Vermeer. And I haven't seen her face, so I can't point her out to you. Sorry. But if you want, you could e-mail that Verhaast guy."

The two Germans stare at each other in frustrated silence. I joined the silence, relishing the lentil soup.

A moment later, the men felt secure enough to discuss their mission in German. Otto wasn't completely satisfied that my appearance in the village was a coincidence, but Hans was impatient to go back up to my room. Otto checked his wristwatch several times, and then made sure his cell phone was on.

It rang in the middle of their discussion what to do with me. He said his name by way of greeting, and then he listen, staring at Hans. When he hung up, he pushed his chair away from the table and simply said in German, "*Der kunstberater* is on his way here. We have to report back in Zurich tomorrow. We'll leave here early in the morning."

"And what about *der kunstberater?*" asked Hans.

"Not for us," said Otto, then added to assuage his colleague, "And as for this idiot, you can do with her whatever you want. I'm going to bed."

I grabbed my computer.

"Why he's coming here?" Hans shot back, standing up.

"I don't know. It's not because he wants to sleep with that one," Otto said, and was gone without a word of goodbye to me.

Without hesitation, Hans bent over my shoulder and whispered, "Esther, sweetheart, shall we continue?"

The bulge in his pants had made its appearance once more.

"Let's eat first. I'm starving. They'll close the kitchen soon," I replied.

"You don't have to send an email to Professor Verhaast. He'll be here tomorrow. Maybe to meet the nun," he said not to inform but to make conversation while he dealt with his erection.

"Yeah." I kept my eyes on the laptop and my trembling hands under the table. I had no contingency plan to deal with Verhaast appearing at the Convent of the Blessed Virgin, but I knew that I had to warn Danielle as soon as I could. Verhaast would identify us. And he might, I realized in horror, catch on to my gambit.

By the time Hans's soup reached our table, I knew how to get rid of him, but not yet how to warn Danielle of Verhaast's appearance. I put my still-trembling hands on Hans's lap under the table and stroked up and down, mostly up. His body quivered, and I attacked the food. He kept his thigh pressed to mine as his hands tore a roll to pieces. His breathing was short and fast, but I ate with gusto. When I was satisfied—the food, I had to admit, wasn't bad—I froze in terror. "Oh shit!" I exclaimed again, frozen in place.

"What now?" he almost wailed.

"Oh shit, oh shit, oh shit!" I cried, afraid to move.

"*What?*"

"I'm gluten intolerant…I forgot to tell them…oh shit, I have to run…ask the nuns for Imodium…I have to run, I have to run!" I grabbed my laptop and bolted out of the restaurant.

Minutes later, Hans knocked on my door. "Esther, sweetheart, I got your medicine."

"Put it outside the door, thank you."

"Are you alright?"

"I'm a mess. You don't want to come in. Go away."

I waited until I no longer heard his footsteps in the corridor, then prepared a cup of coffee in the room's pot and turned on my computer.

I glanced back over my open mail program to see what had been sent. Otto, using my e-mail account, had indeed sent the Hanna Deursen file, but not to Verhaast. He sent it to an address I traced to a website based in Zurich. It belonged to an international insurance company—but now wasn't the time to investigate the cabal.

My thoughts were interrupted when someone knocked on my door, and a female voice called, "Ms. Gutierrez, I'm the house doctor."

I opened the door, and an older nun stepped in. She held the anti-diarrhea medication Hans had left outside the door. Her face wasn't covered, but the rest of her plump body was hidden under her habit. Her eyes registered the cup of coffee, the open laptop, and the room.

"I didn't want to bother with him tonight," I said simply.

She stared at me blankly, and finally said, "I'll pray for you."

"Thank you."

"I take it you have no use to this," she said, waving the medicine.

"No. Thank you," I said.

She shook her head. "Children," she sighed, and gently closed the door behind her.

I hardly slept that night. I called Josh twice, just wanting to hear his voice and his laughter. When I called him the second time and he was worried why I was awake that late, I almost screamed, 'Danielle is alive and well!'—but instinct told me not to do so yet. "I love you, Josh," I said before hanging up.

But mostly, I reread Otto's e-mail to headquarters. Writing in German, he told them, *Attached is Whitmore Verhaast's article, ready for publication. I am waiting for your instructions.*

And I prayed. And I read the paper.

VERHAAST PAPER:

VERMEER SELF PORTRAIT
By:
Whitmore George Verhaast

Fabritius lived down the street from Vermeer.[1]
His house was large, full of light and noise.[2]
Vermeer, by contrast, lived in a small house
that belonged to his restrictive mother-in-law,[3]
a controlled and sober place.[4]

I skipped reading the many footnotes and cross-references I left from Danielle's original paper.

> Fabritius's house was always full of merry crowd, pupils, art dealers, foreign visitors, and apprentices. Some of his visitors were women, most were for fun and play. When Vermeer walked the streets of Delft, it was always on an errand on behalf of his mother-in-law, always alone, his hands clasped behind his back and his face to the cobblestones, but Fabritius whizzed from tavern to tavern like a comet, towing a jolly party along with him.

In the paper I emphasized the sources Danielle had acknowledged, mostly the discoveries by Didrika Margrit Aken, Fredrick William Krinsky, and three other art historians whose fate Danielle didn't specified. Only now Verhaast had made all the discoveries.

> Fabritius was famous; people came to see him from near and far. He studied with Rembrandt in Amsterdam, running the master's workshop until his paintings rivaled the master's and he had to leave Amsterdam. He moved to Delft, bringing with him his reputation and his followers. When the party would enter the tavern that belonged to Vermeer's mother-in-law, Vermeer would watch them from the corner in silence, not daring to join in their singing or even respond to their ribald stories lest his mother-in-law catch him. Vermeer noticed that in the midst of the noisy

entourage was a woman who seldom took part in the party but was always next to Fabritius. Soon, he learned that she was Fabritius's mistress and that she was a painter, a most talented and successful painter in Fabritius's studio. She was beautiful. Her face was open and bright, and her skin reflected warmth and light, her eyes intelligence. She wore a pearl necklace Fabritius had given her and sometimes matching pearl earrings. Her name was Hanna Deursen.

Here, I couldn't resist leaving the source in the body of the paper. In a footnote, Verhaast noted the importance of letters and diaries he (well, Krinsky) discovered in crates stored in the dungeon-like basement of the Convent of the Blessed Virgin.

Vermeer was fascinated by how the light of her skin radiated through the pearls. In short, he was smitten, which emboldened him to tell his mother-in-law that he planned to visit Fabritius's house. His excuse, he told her, was to ask the master for a canvas or two to sell in the tavern and let them make extra money on the commission. Vermeer returned with three canvases and a license to visit Fabritius's house frequently. If anything, his mother-in-law loved a good deal.

Vermeer showed Fabritius sketches he had done in the tavern kitchen when his mother-in-law was away. The master corrected a line here and extended a curve there, and the drawing took on an extra dimension. Fabritius asked his best pupil, Hanna Deursen, to take pity on the young Vermeer and help him with his drawings. "He might amount to something, perhaps in the next world," said Fabritius. Hanna welcomed Vermeer to her work area within the tumultuous activities of Fabritius's workshop. They spent a great deal of time together.

In the early morning hours of October 12, 1654, Vermeer, age twenty-two, married and a father of three, joined his mother-in-law, his wife—pregnant with their fourth child—and his three little children on a trip to visit the bishop in Amsterdam. According to his own writing, he planned to confess his affair with Hanna—not to the bishop but to his wife and mother-in-law—and to declare his love to Hanna. He planned to do so after his mother-in-law had her audience with the bishop, when she would be in her most mellow mood. Less than an hour away from Delft, however, they heard the explosion: the earth shook, the trees bent, the water in the canals rippled, and then they saw clouds of black smoke bellowing above the city. Vermeer jumped off the carriage and ran back to Delft.

Minutes earlier, a clerk with the Dutch Defense garrison stationed in Delft went down to the basement of the city arsenal on his routine rounds, checking the armory. The basement was packed with munitions, explosives, and hundreds of barrels filled with gunpowder. That morning, he had experienced some difficulty inserting the key into the heavy door. To see better, he struck the match he used to light his pipe.

Hundreds died. Thousands more were injured. Half the town was flattened. Body parts were strewn among the rubble. Fabritius was dead, and Vermeer could not find his Hanna.

He returned day after day to the ruins of Fabritius's house, removing bricks and lifting beams. He walked through the many hospitals and infirmaries the government hastily built, peering into bundles of heavily bandaged people on cots and on the ground. His fourth child was born, but he paid little notice. One morning, walking through a courtyard filled with badly injured people whom the doctors had deemed were beyond hope of recovery, he heard a woman whisper, "Johannes."

Vermeer nursed Hanna. He changed her dressing. He entreated doctors to help and bribed nurses to care. Hanna survived, though half her face was blown away, one eye was a black hole, and what remained of her face and body was covered with red blotches, the aftermath of deep burns. She could hardly walk.

Vermeer cajoled his mother-in-law to lend him her carriage; he wanted to repent, he told her, by making the pilgrimage to the Convent of the Blessed Virgin. His mother-in-law smelled redemption. Before dawn the next day, and a year after the explosion, Vermeer whisked his mistress to the convent, then used the annual pilgrimage thereafter as an excuse to visit her. He built her a studio.

Here I added a line in Verhaast's voice: "I'd give half my kingdom to find Hanna Deursen's studio." I couldn't resist inserting his wish in the body of the paper. It was, of course, Danielle's dream.

On his trips back to Delft, Vermeer would carry a painting, sometimes two, put his name on them, and gave them to his mother-in-law to sell in her tavern. On the next trip, he'd give Hanna a receipt, the name of the person who bought each painting, and the amount paid.

Here, Danielle inserted one of her cynical comments, which, of course, I didn't include: "The real Johannes Vermeer was as dry as a grocer; no wonder his mother-in-law wanted him to convert."

The last receipt Vermeer carried with him to the Convent of the Blessed Virgin, dated 1675, never made it into Hanna's hands. She had passed away two months earlier. Vermeer scribbled in the margin that she had left two paintings, one of them a finished self-portrait dedicated to him.

Danielle indicated the number of the last receipt on which Vermeer had scribbled his comment—Krinsky had discovered the receipts and Hanna Deursen's diaries; the last receipt was added to the diaries most likely by the mother superior at the time. Verhaast added.

> There is no indication whether Vermeer took with him the last paintings of Hanna Deursen.

He then concluded his paper with his natural bravura and a flourishing statement I knew only too well:

> Vermeer is not Vermeer. He is a woman by the name of Hanna Deursen. We should—nay, *must*—reevaluate all of Vermeer's paintings."

> Whitmore George Verhaast,
> New Haven 2015.

Danielle had cited Aken's paper on Vermeer. Most likely this was the paper Aken showed Verhaast, which sealed her fate. In the paper she debunked the theory of Vermeer's Camera Obscura, a theory Verhaast had written and opined and of which he made himself the expert. She replaced it with the power of the human brain to adapt to a one-eye sight. Hanna Deursen's brain adjusted to perfection.

I WAS UP IN THE CHAPEL EARLY IN THE MORNING BEFORE THE tram service resumed. I ran all the way up the mountain, watching over my shoulder to see whether I was followed. I knew they would trail me to catch the nun that gave me the flash stick. Given that I had denied knowing the nun's name, I don't know how they thought I would find my benefactress again, but then again, my over-eager German associates hadn't asked too many probing questions about my story.

The chapel was still closed to the public when I arrived, but I pushed the door open. Two nuns tidied the place, replenished the candles, and collected pamphlets. "Your friend will pray at the cemetery this morning," said one.

13

I sprinted to Hanna Deursen's gravestone, but there was no sign of Danielle. I folded my arms and waited, stamping my feet against the cold, and glanced across the cemetery to the tram stop. After fifteen minutes or so, the first tram arrived, and a few people, mostly workers and nuns, disembarked.

And Verhaast.

My heart pounded, and I sprinted away to the gravestones Danielle and I had cleared the day before, up the hill and behind the bend. There, I found her walking along the wall from the other side of the convent.

She had changed. Gone were the hunchback and the limp. Her face was exposed, but she still wore the heavy coverall habit.

"Verhaast is here," I blurted out when she was within earshot.

And as if on cue, we heard Verhaast call, "Sabrina! Come down here!"

We froze.

"For your safety, Sabrina!" he called again, and then in shock and surprise, "Danielle? *Danielle?*" His surprise was genuine, and it turned into a scream. "Danielle, thank God! Wait there!" he ordered, and walked quickly toward us up the hill.

Danielle's eyes widened. "Follow me," she said, and began to run up the slope and along the wall.

We entered the convent compound through a break in the wall that centuries before had been a secret one-horse gate. The compound within the walls was crowded and surprisingly small. The bulky medieval castle that was now the nuns' dorms and the massive church next to the castle occupied most of the space, which seemed abandoned, pocked with moss, an above-ground dungeon embedded in the rocks. Untended shrubs grew wild among the stones. Clotheslines stretched between two arches, loaded with women's coarse undergarments. Danielle yanked garments off the line and ran toward the church. I followed, but she stopped on the threshold.

"Everybody will be in church. Let's hide over there," she said, pointing to a small, windowless stone structure, probably a storage shed, by the wall.

We heard Verhaast call, "For your safety, Danielle! I want to talk to you!"

The shed was empty. Once my eyes adjusted to the dim light, I saw a bench and a table carved out of the rock around which the structure was built. On the far side, behind the stone table, which was part of the convent wall, was a large, dark opening, which at first looked like a fireplace. Danielle tore off her heavy habit, and for a moment, she stood by the stone table in her thong and bra.

"The nuns weren't so crazy about my underwear," she said, remarkably composed as she slipped into her jeans and t-shirt, which she had torn off the clothesline. "I couldn't find my sneakers," she added, tying up the black, shapeless shoes the nuns were wearing. "God, it feels good to wear pants again," she sighed, then saw the shock on my face. "What?"

"Yesterday, you were hysterical, and now you're—"

"I'm going out with you. Changed tactics. Sabrina, I was wrong." She held my hands and spoke as if in a trance. "I should have gone public, instead of running away. *Fuck* Verhaast!"

I understood her line of reasoning, which, on its own, was logical. The mistake that Krinsky and Didrika and Isidor had made was dealing one-on-one with Verhaast. Had they published their findings, the cabal would have been less audacious.

"I already e-mailed my mother to tell her I'm coming home," she said happily. "Here, take my picture," she said, lounging on the stone table.

She was euphoric to have found way out of the trap, almost drunk with joy. In contrast, I felt my plan shatter.

"Come on, Sabrina, take a picture!" she insisted. "You have your iPhone, right?"

I needed time to think, and so I snapped a picture. The flash went off.

"Danielle!" we heard Verhaast call.

He had seen the flash.

"Fuck!" exclaimed Danielle, and jumped behind the stone table and into the fireplace to hide. "Wow," she cried, "check it out! It's not a fireplace." She disappeared.

I heard Verhaast running over the rocks, and so I jumped into the opening after Danielle.

THE TUNNEL WAS PITCH-BLACK. I heard Danielle crawling, and I crawled quickly after her. The tunnel soon gave way to a cave, and the floor began to descend, stretching the space until the roof was no longer mere inches over my head. Still, the breathing room wasn't much help against the cold and the dark.

"Sabrina?" Danielle whispered, coming to a sudden stop. I bumped into her, and she tapped my arm. "Give me your phone."

I fumbled in my pocket, afraid to admit that I was scared and had no idea where we were, and handed her the phone. With a few taps, she found the flashlight app and illuminated a set of steps. "Good," she said, and I heard her walking down the spiral steps.

I yearned for the surface—it felt like we were going down a well—but Danielle refused to listen to my protestations. "There's got to be a way out of here. Those birds didn't come from the shed," she said, and pointed to the far wall, where a pair of small birds sat on a rock ledge.

Frankly, I was scared, and Danielle was beyond control. I had no idea how long we'd descended when I felt that I no longer needed to lean on the tunnel walls for balance. Finally, after an eternity of walking through the shadows, Danielle pointed the light at a door, then pushed on it without hesitation. "Help me," she whispered.

The door was heavy, oak banded with iron, and obviously hadn't been opened for centuries. Once we nudged it a crack, the smell hit us first—not offensive or stuffy, but sharp and distinguished. And then we saw the light.

"Wow," said Danielle.

We stood on the threshold of a large cave. The morning sun filtered in through trees and a thicket growing on the other side of a window, which was but a cut through the rock. Opposite the window, across the cave, I saw an opening. No light penetrated in, but I sensed the outdoors and began to breathe again.

"Sabrina," Danielle whispered, "we've entered a Vermeer painting."

Only then did I see the furniture. The heavy draperies and the tablecloths. The globe. The white pitchers. The map and the tapestry on the wall. The virginal by the window. A four-poster bed. The canopy sagging but still blue. A canvas-shaped object on a large easel, covered by what once was white cloth. Brushes and containers littered the room, stained by paint dried centuries ago.

"Sabrina," Danielle whispered, either shocked or in awe. "This is Hanna Deursen's studio."

I pointed at the only painting on the wall: one of Fabritius's self-portraits. It wasn't finished, yet it was in a frame.

He was winking and wore a half-smile of pleasure and satisfaction under ruddy cheeks. "She painted him," whispered Danielle, taking a step sideways and then forward, and then she stopped, wide-eyed and delirious.

A guidebook at the museum had mentioned that the first settlement on the convent's site had been a castle and chapel built by retreating tenth-century crusaders. The tunnel into the cave must have been their escape route in case their enemies crept west. And centuries later, I surmised, Vermeer built a studio in there for his Hanna. And there, she hung the painting of the man she loved.

The cloth that covered the painting on the easel was covered with a thick layer of dust and bird droppings—in fact, the whole studio was caked with dung and nests, and, I saw with a little shudder, tiny bones.

"This is amazing," Danielle whispered, oblivious to the decay around her. "It's unbelievable—"

"Hanna Deursen's studio," cried Verhaast.

He stood by the door through which we'd come, his face the picture of astonishment.

"It's unbelievable," Danielle replied, as if she had expected Verhaast all along.

Verhaast shook with excitement, and Danielle beamed.

Danielle whispered, "This is the setting of *The Art Lesson*."

"Maybe. Yes. It is. Don't touch anything."

They stared at the covered painting with the reverence of a high priest and priestess before opening the ark. "Don't touch *anything*," Verhaast whispered again like a prayer.

"The water pitcher," Danielle said, still in a daze, pointing at the jug on the virginal.

"Take a picture," he said finally.

She snapped shots with my phone, again and again.

Gradually, she became more disciplined, but continued to photograph every inch of the room. At one point, Verhaast stood by the virginal as if looking out the window and instructed her to take his picture. He knew exactly where to stand so that the light washed his face—just like the women by the window in Vermeer's paintings. Danielle snapped.

"Now take my picture," she said, handing him the phone.

But Verhaast put my phone in his pocket and smiled.

He never so much as looked in my direction. In their euphoria, I had ceased to exist.

THE SIGNIFICANCE OF THIS DISCOVERY DIDN'T ESCAPE ME, BUT proving that Vermeer was a deformed woman wasn't my objective. Verhaast and Danielle continued to discuss their findings; he gradually turned into his opportunistic academician self, and Danielle into his supplicant student-collaborator. Only after long minutes did Danielle think to call for me.

By then, I wasn't in the studio. I had stepped out through the opening in the wall behind the four-poster bed, and I sat on a ledge that once was a step into the cave, surveying the path through the woods. The flora had encroached upon the ledge over time, but I could imagine that this had been the path poor Vermeer had traveled to visit his Hanna.

Inside, the art historians were in a trance, speculating about whether *The Kitchen Maid* was set by the window, or *Woman Reading a Letter*, or *Woman Holding a Balance*—Danielle had discovered a balance on a table—or *Woman with a Pearl Necklace*. "The necklace!" I heard Verhaast exclaim, most likely discovering a pearl necklace next to a mirror. I wondered when it would dawn on these two art historians that the window was the same window* in all the paintings, that the settings of all the paintings were this room-studio, and that Deursen never left this cave. Here she encountered the snake she included in *The Allegory of Faith,* and the globe, most likely Vermeer had retrieved and carried from Delft, was the globe in her painting *The Astronomer.* In her last painting, her self-portrait hanging among blacksmith's tools in an antiques store in Bazel, Deursen had painfully recorded every item in the studio, bidding farewell to the room and most likely to her life. She had dedicated the painting to her benefactor, a poor tavern owner by the name of Johannes Vermeer.

The Astronomer by Johannes Vermeer

But that wasn't my concern.

I heard Verhaast lecture Danielle about how to inform the academic community, and then the world, of their discovery. "First, I have to establish that Vermeer is Hanna Deursen," he said.

"I've already done that," said Danielle.

"Yes, yes, yes, we'll publish it," he mumbled. "Then this room, it should be documented with professional cameras,

---

* See Historical Art Notes on page 167.

item by item in detail. And this canvas. I'll remove the
cover on camera. I'll reveal to the world a new Vermeer-
slash-Deursen." He couldn't stop himself.

Poor Danielle wasn't aware that for him, the discovery
wasn't enough. He was already planning his triumphal
parade into history, and I didn't think that Danielle could
sense that she wouldn't be standing next to him.

But that wasn't my concern.

Danielle's safety was.

Sitting on the ledge outside Deursen's studio, I knew
my plan was on the verge of collapse. At that moment, I
had no idea whether my attempt to deflect the cabal's
attention from Danielle to Verhaast had succeeded. But I
knew that our lives, Danielle's and mine, were in danger—if
not from the cabal, then from Verhaast. It was now in his
interest to let the cabal deal with Danielle and me. Once
his witnesses were off the stage—Danielle, after all, had
disappeared weeks ago—he would make his splash. Surely
he knew that he should make his entrance publicly, noisily,
with fanfare and flourish worthy of a triumphal Caesar's
parade—and thus eclipse the cabal. Vermeer's paintings
would go through reevaluation, and Verhaast would be the
only arbiter.

No wonder he was ecstatic.

I overheard his plans to haul photography equipment,
high-density lights, projectors, and reflecting screens
through the convent. "We'll need generators," said Danielle. She was still talking as a partner, whereas Verhaast
used solely 'me' and 'I.'

"I'll see to it," he replied.

Danielle, to my surprise, injected words of caution:
"Won't *they* stop us?"

"Who are *they*?" he asked, suddenly on guard.

"The people you warned me—"

"Stop. That never happened."

"But it did. I had to hide—"

"Did you? You couldn't have been hiding very well if *Sabrina* found you."

"She's the smartest person I know," Danielle replied in a huff.

"Is she?"

"*You* should know. You hurt her—"

He either slapped her or shook her by the arms, hissing, "Stop this nonsense right now if you ever want to leave this place!"

There was a long stretch of silence. I heard Verhaast clear his throat, trying to speak, and finally I heard him say softly, "I'm sorry, Danielle. All of this here…it's amazing, overwhelming. Besides, what's Sabrina to you? She's just holding you back."

"She's my friend."

He had the sense not to challenge her. I, too, detected her conviction. Instead, he resumed discussing Deursen's studio and her paintings. "And you *do* understand why it should be kept secret until this room is documented?" he injected at one point. I couldn't hear her reply, but I heard his sudden angry call: "Sabrina!"

Of course, I, too, should be dealt with.

"Sabrina!" he repeated.

I didn't reveal my presence.

"She probably went back to the inn," said Danielle, and Verhaast gave up.

I HAVE NO IDEA HOW long I sat on the ledge. I imagined poor Vermeer trekking his way up the overgrown path to visit his Hanna, or walking back down the hill to Delft carrying a canvas or two. Did they hug? Did he kiss her? I hoped for him that she had exaggerated her deformity in the painting of her portrait. Did he glance at Fabritius's portrait? Every once in a while, a flash went off in the cave, Verhaast documenting the find of four centuries—on my smartphone. Their conversation faded away from my attention, though I was affected by their excitement.

I heard Verhaast speculate, "Most likely, Krinsky didn't find the studio. He wouldn't leave this canvas on the easel." This was followed by a flash.

Danielle was eager to see the covered painting. Verhaast blocked her, sometimes rudely. He wanted his reaction on camera to be genuine. "I'll do it live on TV," he said, and later, "I have to find a way to preserve the studio as-is. Tourists will trample the place…I'll build a special museum and a replica of the studio—"

THE LEAVES CHANGED SHADES IN the gentle breeze that came up from the village, twisting between dark green and the bright color of new growth, as if invisible hands shook a carpet. When Verhaast stepped out of the cave, I hid quickly behind a bush. He surveyed the terrain, snapped a picture, and puffed his chest. I could imagine him pounding his chest like Tarzan, and then I saw him unzip his fly and urinate. When he finished, he snapped another picture and reentered the cave. I thought with a delightful whiff that if he blew up the picture, he would see me peering at him from behind the bush. I smiled to myself and hoped I had smiled when he snapped the picture.

Danielle, taking her turn, stepped out to pee. I moved, alerting her to my presence. She winked at me, quickly put her finger on her mouth—*keep quiet*—and walked back in. I was relieved that she wasn't, after all, in Verhaast's grip.

Soon, I lost interest in Vermeer, and thought about my failing plot to punish Verhaast—and lost interest in that as well. I thought of Josh. Not his part in the plot—I had no doubt that he would have two tickets back to the States waiting for Danielle and me at the airport and that he would wait for us at JFK. I thought back to the first time I had consented to his relentless pursuit to have dinner with him in the dining hall. *"It's not a date, Sabrina. Let's just talk,"* he had entreated. I felt then that he didn't take me as a dumb Latina. And suddenly, I wanted to be with him. To hear his tireless linear logic with no leaps or associations. And realized that I had loved him long before I knew I was in love with him, and that for a long time, I had held myself back. Him, a trust-fund kid. Me, a fat Latina on full scholarship. He couldn't stop from talking about his family, grandparents, cousins, uncles, and aunts, all close and funny. Me—well, I told him about my mother. Of course, I hadn't told him about the circumstance of my birth or my rape, and certainly not about the abortion. And now, I wished he were next to me.

While I stared into space, I thought of myself as a chubby second grader with frizzled hair. I was sent home from school with lice, and the teacher didn't care that my mother was at work and that there was no one to open the door for me. But Josh, good and dependable Josh, would be there when I got back to the States. Verhaast faded away, was no longer important or worth my time.

Watching the wind play with the leaves, I mused that if not for Danielle's disappearance, I would have mentally sent Verhaast to hell, forgotten about my pain, and concentrated on graduate schools, and wouldn't have taken Josh for granted. Long shadows had descended on the gorge; only the tips of the mountains were awash in the setting sun—and I noticed that it had been a while since I had heard Danielle and Verhaast, and that the day was dimming.

I ENTERED THE CAVE AND removed the cloth that covered the canvas on the easel.

The most beautiful woman of all Vermeer's women stared directly at me. Her face radiated light. Her eyes were dark brown, soft and warm, and she had a gentle and inviting smile. Her bare shoulders were smooth and slender. She wore a pair of pearl earrings and a pearl necklace that I couldn't take my eyes away. Her left hand softly touched the left earring, and her lovely head slightly tilted to meet the hand, either to take the earring off or put it back on. The necklace rested on her voluptuous cleavage. Verhaast loved to point out in his lectures and writings that Vermeer's women were comfortable and demure in their domestic settings, void of passion or seduction. This woman by contrast had just made love or was about to join her lover in bed, and she relished the moment.

A dedication and a signature were on the bottom left of the canvas, but it was already too dark in the cave to read.

Before lifting the painting off the easel, I glanced at the portrait of Carel Fabritius. He, too, had just made love or was about to do so.

I CAREFULLY PUT THE PAINTING in the trunk of my rental car before entering the inn, and I went directly to my room.

The walk back to the inn was longer and more difficult than I had anticipated. The shrubs were dense, and in places, I had to climb over hanging rocks to circumvent especially thick clusters, all the while holding and protecting Hanna Deursen's last painting, much as, I imagined, Vermeer had done four centuries ago.

When I left the ledge, the light was sufficient for me to read the line and see the signature. Once again, I was struck by how beautiful the woman was. The letters were drawn clearly and with great care:

To Iohannes when I loved Carel
Hanna Deursen, 1675

Poor Vermeer. Now he seemed even more pathetic than heroic. I wondered where he would stop to put his signature on the paintings—here, before reaching the village, or in the back of his mother's-in-law tavern before hanging them for sale. *Was Hanna Deursen's signature the reason he left this painting on the easel? Or Carl Fabritius's mocking smile?* After his last visit, he walked back to Delft empty-handed and with an empty heart.

He died shortly thereafter.

Self-Portrait by Carel Fabrituius

I FINISHED QUICKLY WASHING UP IN MY ROOM, GRABBED MY COM-
puter, and rushed down to the dining hall to use the lobby's WiFi to communicate with Josh. I was also starving.

"Sabrina, please join me," Verhaast called as soon as I
entered the inn's restaurant.

"Where's Danielle?" I asked, not covering my alarm.

"She's collecting her stuff from the convent," he said
as if they had discussed and planned the rest of the evening. "Where have you been? We were looking for you,"
he said, turning his legal pad, which he had filled with
pages of intoxicating writing, upside-down. His black turtleneck and brown tweed jacket were as always impeccable,
his back straight and his face aglow, and his eyes reflected
victory. "I hope you realize
the significance of my... of
this finding," he said, and
I heard the doubt in his
voice as to whether the
fat Latina was capable of
grasping its magnitude.

"May I have my
phone back?" I asked,
still standing by the
table.

"Oh, yes, Danielle mentioned it was yours," he said, placing it in the middle of the table. "Sit down, Sabrina, I want to talk with you. As a matter of fact, both Danielle and I want to talk with you."

I picked up my phone eager to check my messages.

"By the way, you don't have to worry about space on the phone. I transferred all the pictures to my computer and deleted them from your phone. Sit, down, Sabrina, please."

The nun-waitress that came to take my order helped me cover up the tremor in my stomach. All the way from the cave to the inn, I thought that the painting and the pictures on my phone would give Danielle the punch she would need to prove that she was part of the discovery. Now the pictures were lost. I ordered dinner and sat as far away from Verhaast at the round table as I could.

"Charge her dinner to me," he said to the nun-waitress, and ordered a bottle of red wine. He obviously felt good about himself.

I skimmed quickly over Josh's numerous messages and quickly texted to him back. It had been a long day without communication. Josh answered almost instantaneously, and I was grateful that the phone was on mute. Verhaast was lecturing. I was his only audience, yet he was lecturing about the revolution *his* discovery would bring to the art world. After I assured Josh that I was okay and he texted back his relief, I turned off my phone and cut Verhaast off midsentence.

"I know all that, I read your paper," I said, buttering a fresh roll.

"My paper?"

"Yes. I have it on my computer," I replied, and took a big bite of the roll.

While he expressed astonishment and confusion, I turned on my computer and brought up the paper. He read, his face paling, and I enjoyed my dinner.

"Very clever, very clever," he murmured every once in a while, but didn't stop reading. "Very clever indeed," he declared through clenched teeth when he finished. He stared at me, eyes ablaze. Most likely, he had already figured out how to get rid of me. His lower lip trembled in fury. I poured myself a glass of wine. "And you think you can get away with it," he hissed.

I didn't bother to answer before I sipped the wine. "Excellent choice," I said to him.

"You little cunt—"

"Yes, you've already told me that," I said, cutting my steak.

"You have nothing," he said. "I deleted the article from your computer."

"That's okay," I answered, and for the first time looked directly at him. "I've already sent it to Zurich. Well, *I* didn't— my new friend Otto did. I think you two have met. You're working for them, aren't you?" I added with my mouth full.

His transformation was so sudden that I expected him to collapse to the floor any minute. "You didn't," he labored. "How dare you...You didn't—"

"Yes, I did," I said, enjoying staring directly at him.

"You little... you... you..."

"I know. You've told me," I said, and continued my dinner.

He recovered enough to sip some wine, collecting his thoughts. Then he speculated aloud that tomorrow morning he would go public with the discovery. Or better yet, as soon as Danielle joined him, they would compose a statement. I noticed that it was the first time he had included Danielle in his plans. Or better yet, he would call the authorities to secure the studio and the convent—he would do it as soon as the offices were open in the morning.

I finished my dinner while he was still talking, and then I noticed a couple of German tourists approaching our table. When they arrived, the woman gushed as if meeting a celebrity. "*Sie sind* Professor Verhaast, yes?" she called, as if asking for his autograph.

Verhaast was ready for a moment of adulation, but then he recognized the woman's "husband," and his smile vanished. A brief exchange in German ensued, and it quickly dawned on Verhaast that it was futile to resist.

"Let me take my computer," he said, standing up.

"We already have it," said the woman.

He collected his notes and joined the couple, pretending that it was a friendly and familiar outing.

I ordered desert, Belgian waffles with three scoops of ice cream.

"WHO ARE THOSE PEOPLE WALKING out with Verhaast?" Danielle said even before she reached my table.

"Probably the same people who picked up Krinsky and Aken," I replied.

She froze, and I let it sink in. We locked eyes for a brief moment that seemed like forever.

"How the hell did you manage that?" she whispered.

I fished the paper out from the trash bin and turned the computer to her. Then I filled my glass with wine and poured one for Danielle while she was reading.

First I saw fear in her hazel eyes, and I expected panic. To my relief, she slowly closed the laptop, still reflecting on the consequences, and picked up her wine. "You're crazy," she whispered, raising the glass in silent salute.

Silence.

Then we burst out laughing, startling the nuns on duty and the few guests in the restaurant. But we didn't care. It was laughter of acknowledgement and relief and triumph.

And Danielle began to talk.

I often wonder about the degree of subtle communication between roommates who are also close friends. No words are needed to exchange to explain feelings or thoughts. For instance, during spring semester of our junior year Danielle entered the dining hall with a tall, broad-shouldered varsity swimmer, a senior secret society type. They joined Josh and me for supper. We had a pleasant time; it was a happy table. The next morning, Danielle commented, "You don't like Mitch, do you, huh?" She just knew.

And such was the case that evening. We didn't have to explain or complete sentences or go over the sequence of events or speculate on consequences. We knew. We understood each other. She was giddy and jumped from subject to subject like a pinball. I didn't have any problem following. She speculated about Verhaast and his fate. Her paper. Her book. The New Vermeer. In between and not in sequence, she inserted bits of the conversation she had had earlier with her parents. Her father would put the legal department of his corporation onto checking whether she had broken the law, and if so, how to get out of the charges. She would have some explaining to do to Yale's Executive Committee as well, which might suspend her for a semester. "Good," she added, "I'll have time to write the book." She planned to take Isidor to the Met.

"Together," I said.

"Sure. Or we might pull a reverse heist. Take the Isidor out and replace it with the Vermeer. You plan it."

"The Hanna Deursen, you mean."

"Exactly."

We laughed, and then we finished the bottle of wine. The restaurant was empty, the nuns were gone, and Danielle was sounding like a kidnapped girl kept in isolation and suddenly free to talk and sing and laugh. I contributed to the conversation little, but at one point, with no clear connection, I blurted out, "I think I'm in love with Josh."

"Girl," she replied without a second's hesitation, "you were the only one who didn't know that," and continued to speculate about the self-portrait of the mangled woman. "I would visit her," she said, and once again mentioned Isidor. We both noted that we were inebriated, but we could not stop.

"Wow, girl," she exclaimed after an hour, "I better go back before they lock the door. See you at breakfast," she added, and jogged for the door.

"Josh texted me about a one o'clock flight," I called after her.

She just waved and ran out of the empty restaurant.

I HAD SEEN DANIELLE IN a rage only once. It was during finals of fall semester freshman year and just before the winter recess. We didn't know each other then—well, she certainly didn't know me, though I knew of her. I sat at the last table near the service area and had a view of the entire dining hall. The sudden brisk movement at the entrance drew my attention. Danielle whisked by the ID-swipe lady at the counter without a blink. Two students chatting in the aisle stepped out of her way in a hurry. Like a laser-guided missile, she reached the senior table, then faced a guy who had just raised his head to see her incoming. She was mad, trembling with anger, and pointed her finger at him. After saying something I couldn't hear, and without skipping one heartbeat, she grabbed the cup of water in front of him and threw his drink in his face. With that, she turned and walked out of the dining hall with the same lightning speed, nodding an apology to the ID-swipe lady as she passed. Some people catcalled, some applauded, and most were laughing, enjoying the scene.

I never learned the cause of her anger—it was over and forgotten. But I remembered her face. Set, determined, and without fear, and above all, the rage in her eyes.

I saw this rage again the next morning at breakfast.

I had slept very little that night, instead mostly chatting with Josh. Halfway through our conversation, I noticed that we were talking as if we had been a couple for years, set in our relationship and comfortable. It spread warmth in my chest. In the morning, I packed, checked out, and waited for Danielle.

As soon as I entered the lobby, I felt that something had happened during the night. The nun at the desk confirmed my fears: there had been a fire near the convent. She said they hadn't had a brush fire in decades, but they prayed and the fire subsided. "Probably rowdy teenagers," she said. "I pray nobody is hurt."

I wanted to ask more questions, but then I saw Danielle entering the lobby, and I recalled the fury in her eyes. She walked directly to me and pointed her finger at my chest.

"Did you tell them about the studio?"

"No," I said.

She turned and walked out of the lobby.

"Danielle," I called, but she was already gone.

Ten minutes later, she texted me that she had decided to stay, she might visit the antique store in Bazel, and I shouldn't wait for her. To my relief, she did sign with her customary "Hugs and XOXO."

JOSH PICKED ME UP AT JFK. "Where's Danielle?" he asked between kisses.

"I don't know," I whispered. He stared at me, and I finally said, "It's a long story."

It was the first time I was grateful for the traffic congestion on I-95 to New Haven. I started with the rape and the abortion—not a single word was a lie—and ended with, "For the life of me, I don't know how the cabal thugs learned about Hanna Deursen's studio."

"I told them," he said.

"*You?*"

He laughed. His laughter had a touch of a condescending edge to it, but I let it go. "Your laptop was my cue," he explained. "First, you asked me to crack a password, and then you told you should replace same computer—only now, it was Danielle's. You took my computer, which automatically backs up onto iCloud. Then you connected your iPhone to the computer." He shrugged. "I read Danielle's paper on Hanna Deursen, and then I read the same paper in Verhaast's voice that you sent to an address in Zurich. I saw the pictures you took on your iPhone, and then there was nothing. Not a text, not a call." He paused, pretending to be busy with the traffic, then added simply, "I sent the pictures to the address in Zurich where you sent the paper."

"What made you do that?"

"Because of your preface to Verhaast's paper." He quoted in badly accented German, "*Attached is Whitmore Verhaast's article, ready for publication. I am waiting for your instructions.*"

He paused again, now waiting for my reaction, but none came. I was speechless and most likely breathless.

And then he murmured, "And also because I love you, and because you'll be my wife someday."

Afterword

WHILE DANIELLE'S RETURN SOLVED ONE MYSTERY, ANOTHER had developed overnight: where in the world was Whitmore Verhaast? After no one heard from him for weeks, the police entered his house and riffled through his belongings, looking for hints of foul play. Nothing was ever found. Verhaast had taken his wallet and passport, though there was no indication that he had ever left the country. (I could only guess at the many passports and aliases Verhaast used, but I didn't tell that to the police. And Danielle, for once, learned to keep her mouth shut.) His TAs finished teaching his spring courses in his absence, and when he had yet to call by May, the art history department moved his office's contents into storage. I had accompanied Danielle to see her new thesis adviser that afternoon and was just in time to see Verhaast's leather couch being wheeled away, into a basement somewhere and out of my life.

AND WHAT WAS TO BE said of Danielle's thesis? Her new adviser, Morgan Thorne, had his own connections, and he sent it and all her attached sources to the director of the Met with "Read ASAP" scrawled in red Sharpie across the envelope. The Met—and, for that matter, the larger artistic community—wasn't entirely sold on her conclusion by the time her thesis was submitted. The two canvases of *Young Woman with a Water Pitcher*, Isidor's and the Vermeer-Deursen's, were still under evaluation, but she had been promised the cover story in the June issue of *Smithsonian*. She was also busy with the meticulous processes required to authenticate Deursen's self portrait. Her father had failed to buy the painting, but Walker Mendelssohn had a private conversation with the Mertens, Krinsky's daughter and son-in-law, and flew back to the U.S. with the painting. He disclosed very little of what had transpired in the conversation or whether he had paid a cent for the canvas, but he gave it to Danielle as a thank-you gift from his father.

AS FOR ME, I GRADUATED *magna cum laude*, two-tenths of a grade point shy of *summa*. Considering I'd worried myself sick all fall and taken no classes all spring, I thought that was fair. My mother was radiant, eager to tell anyone within earshot that I was her daughter and that she could not be prouder. When the dean called my name as part of a small group of inductees to Phi Beta Kappa, I stood for nobody else but her. Josh's older brother was prancing around with a zillion-dollar camera, shooting pictures as if I were already part of the family.

We made it to dinner with the Carruthers after all, and our parents raised a toast to our next steps: Danielle would be back at the Met while pursuing a PhD at Columbia, while I, thanks to some help from the Mendelssohns, would actually get to spend a few months at the Keck Observatory in Hawaii before deciding whether an astronomy PhD was in my future.

Josh had already requested that if I should opt for the grad school route, I choose the University of Hawaii at Manoa. "After years of New England cold, I'd like to follow you somewhere tropical," he explained.

We hadn't seriously spoken of marriage yet, but I must admit, I'd begun to entertain thoughts of a barefoot wedding on the beach. The cynical part of me insisted that anyone would give free rein to fantasies just prior to moving to paradise with one's boyfriend, but the part of my mind that lay deeper and spoke only the truth told me Josh would follow me up the side of Mauna Kea if I needed him.

He knew everything, and he still loved me. And for that, I could only love him more.

I MADE MY FINAL METRO-NORTH trip to New York the day after graduation. I knocked on Isidor's door and beamed when it unlatched. He embraced me, congratulated me on a successful trip, and exhorted me to call him from Hawaii. I promised, and as he brought out tea, I took a cloth-wrapped canvas from my leather backpack.

"I found this in Belgium," I said, watching his face as the beautiful Hanna was revealed. "It's in need of restoration, but I wouldn't trust just anybody with a Deursen. Do you know of someone who might be interested?"

He brushed his fingertips over Hanna's dark waves, then looked up at me and smiled. "Why, yes, Sabrina," he murmured. "I know a fellow who has experience with Vermeers."

Historical Art Notes

FROM THE BOOK:

I wondered when it would dawn on these two
art historians that the window was the same
window in all the paintings, that the settings
of all the paintings were this room-studio, and
that Deursen never left this cave. Here she
encountered the snake she included in *The
Allegory of Faith*, and the globe, most likely
Vermeer had retrieved and carried from Delft,
was the globe in her painting *The Astronomer*.

Christ in the House of Martha and Mary by Johannes Vermeer

Girl Reading a Letter by an Open Window by Johannes Vermeer

The Milkmaid by Johannes Vermeer

Woman in Blue Reading a Letter by Johannes Vermeer

Young Woman with a Pearl Necklace by Johannes Vermeer

Woman Holding a Balance by Johannes Vermeer

The Art of Painting by Johannes Vermeer

List of Illustrations

DEC 0 8 2015

CPSIA information can be obtained
at www.ICGtesting.com
Printed in the USA
LVOW02s1630181115
463166LV00014B/61/P